Vicious Sinners

Devious Secrets

MEASHA STONE

DEVIOUS SECRETS
VICIOUS SINNERS
BOOK I

MEASHA STONE

VICIOUS SINNERS

Devious Secrets
Devious Madness
Devious Truth
Devious Corruption
Devious Revenge
Devious Obsession

Copyright © 2025 by Black Heart Publications and Measha Stone
All rights reserved. No part of this book may be reproduced or transmitted in any form or by any means, electronic or mechanical, including photocopying, recording, or by any information storage and retrieval system, without permission in writing from the publisher.

Published by Black Heart Publications, LLC

Stone, Measha
Devious Secrets

Cover Design by Deranged Doctor Design

This book is intended for *adults only*. Spanking and other sexual activities represented in this book are fantasies only, intended for adults.

ONE

MEGAN

Adjusting the catering vest I'd swiped from the supply cart, I balance a tray of champagne and try to pretend my entire life doesn't depend on making it through the next door unnoticed.

Men in expensive tailored suits filling the air with thick cigar smoke crowd the cavernous antechamber. Dim sconces cast pools of amber light, their electric flames barely strong enough to reach the vaulted ceiling, giving the space an even more ominous feel. Heavy wooden doors, reinforced with iron, loom at the far end—just behind them is my prize. The reason for this insane visit.

A single figure stands at the entrance, half-hidden in shadow, watching the room. He lifts his glass to his lips and a bit of light hits his knuckle where a heavy ring sits. My throat tightens when I recognize the shape. It's a skull.

Gliding my gaze up from the glass, his gaze locks with mine. It's only a moment. A fleeting second, but my breath catches. As quickly as he noticed me, his attention flickers away, his jaw tightening as though whatever he's seeing is annoying him.

I slide behind three men huddled together, muttering to each other in a foreign language before he finds me again. Just as I turn to head back toward the front entrance of the room, a member of the waitstaff—an actual member, not someone posing like myself—breezes by with an ashtray. I freeze and turn to the left. My heart is hammering so hard against my ribs, I'm not sure I'll ever be able to breathe comfortably again after tonight.

"Ah, I'll take one of those." A hand appears out of another huddled group and one of the three glasses on my tray disappears.

"Gentlemen. The auction is set to begin shortly. Please make your way down to the lounge and ready your wallets," a deep voice carries over the room.

The heavy wooden doors creak as they open, and the men in the room file out, headed toward whatever debauchery this place offers.

Once the room is cleared, I leave my tray on a table and slip through the doors. My nerves settle a fraction now that I'm inside. The information I'd been given could have been complete bullshit. This whole thing could be a setup.

Taking a calming breath and reminding myself of how much I need to get through this, I put my focus on the task at hand.

Like the antechamber, the corridor before me is dimly lit with electric sconces on the thick brick walls. My rubber-soled flats make no sound against the cement flooring as I make my way toward what I hope is the office I'm looking for at the end of the hall.

A light flickers at the end and voices echo against the

stone. Flattening myself against the chilled brick, I freeze. There's nowhere to hide in this corridor.

Dammit. Shoes click, and the voices get a little louder. If I hurry, I might be able to get back into the antechamber before I'm seen. Fear paralyzes me, and I stay flattened against the brick when someone laughs.

"We're going to be late, and the girl I want is up soon." Another laugh fades as the footsteps move away from my spot. They're headed somewhere else. My lungs start working again.

His words give me pause. The girl he wants is up soon? What does that mean exactly? I glance around my surroundings, knowing I'm in unauthorized territory belonging to the Volkov family. This hallway should lead me to their offices, but there's something more sinister about this place than just offices.

And what did that man mean by what he said?

Don't get caught up in the details. Get what you came for and get the hell out.

I need to hurry. The sooner I get this done, the faster I can finally sleep through the night without a panic attack. I would give almost anything for things to go back to how they were months ago. When I could curl up on the couch with my best friend for a night of bad movies, cheap wine, and takeout instead of lurking around secret mafia clubs, trying to save our lives.

Rushing to the end of the corridor, I find a foyer of sorts that splits off into two more hallways, all lit with the dim light of the sconces, no real markings as to what lies in either direction.

I grit my teeth.

What if my intel is wrong? What if I'm running right into a

trap that's going to make my life even more messed up than it was when I woke up this morning.

Panic kicks my heartbeat into a gallop.

Calm down.

Taking several more calming breaths, I try to remember what the strange man on the phone said. The hall to the... left? Right? Dammit!

Ugh! The right. He said right. Completely unsure of my decision, I turn down the hallway to my right.

The doorknob of the first door I come to is unlocked, so I softly push the arched wooden door until I can slip inside and shut it. It's dark, but I find the switch for the lights easily on the wall.

Whoa.

I've never seen anything so beautiful before. The chandelier dangling in the center of the room is wrought iron with twelve electric candles planted around the circumference. It's suspended by a thick black link chain. The room is much the same sophisticated, elegant style. Thick dark wood shelves are lined with aged leather books.

A desk with rolled edges and thick legs that look painstakingly elegant with carvings to make them look like pillars sits in the middle of the room. Nothing other than a leather desk blotter, the top of the desk is clear.

As beautiful as the room is, I don't see any file cabinets. What I'm looking for would be in a file folder.

I think.

My neck becomes slick with sweat as I try to remember every detail I was given. This is the room. At least it matches the description right down to the brown leather couches in the corner of the room.

Books. He said something about what I needed to find would be behind books. Or in a book? It would have been great if I'd been able to keep the notes I scribbled down, but the voice had been adamant not to bring anything that would make it harder to explain if I was caught.

Because if I'm caught, I'm on my own. There's no one to throw under the bus who can help me. Revealing anything would trigger unsurmountable danger.

Checking out the bookcase, I realize there's something odd about the books lined up. Other than there's a worrisome number of books on war, they are all perfectly in line. Not a single book is any larger than the one beside it, but they aren't a collection that would explain the uniformity.

My hand trembles when I reach up to run my fingers over the bindings of the books. One book has a different feel to the leather. It's softer. More supple.

It moves easily when I wiggle it from its place. There's a metallic snap from behind the book and then it's stuck. It won't come any farther out. The other books, all fold down still in a perfect line.

They aren't books at all. It's a panel disguising a cabinet behind it. My chest can barely contain my heart, it's pounding so hard.

This has to be it.

There doesn't seem to be any locks or combinations on the cabinet door. It opens right away when I pull the black metal handle.

Clear plastic containers are lined up, double stacked. Each labeled with a name. My eyes flick from one to the next, looking for the name I need. Luckily, they're in alphabetical order.

At least the criminals are organized.

Most of these names are easily recognizable. Jasper Cunnings, I saw his name flash across the news headlines as I was scrolling my phone yesterday. He's some politician.

Most of these little boxes have political figures' names on them.

Finally, my eyes land on the one I'm looking for.

Dexter Thompson.

I grab hold of the box and pry open the lid. Inside are photographs, a flash drive, and a set of small keys that look like they're for a safe deposit box.

Curious, I pick up one of the photographs and turn it over. Dexter Thompson, I assume—I've never seen him before—sits with his legs spread in a chair. He's naked. And so is the woman kneeling between his knees. She's bound, with her hands behind her back and her ankles zip-tied together.

Tears stain her cheeks as she looks up at him. Her mascara's run with her tears.

There's a wedding band on Dexter's finger, but I'm assuming this isn't his wife in the photograph.

"What the hell are you doing in here?" a voice booms behind me.

Shit!

In my surprise, I spin around. The box slips from my hand in my hurry and hits the ground, spilling the contents everywhere.

"I... uh..." I look down at the box. "It was an accident. I was...Um, I wasn't..."

The man, dressed in a black suit with a narrow black tie over his white button-down shirt and an earpiece tucked into his left ear, stomps over to me.

We both reach for the box at the same time, but he snaps it up before me. The drive is by my foot. I cover it with the toe of my shoe and drag it closer to me. When he turns to the bookcase to grab the lid for the box, I quickly snatch up the drive and shove it into my bra.

He pushes the lid back on the box, not noticing my movements.

"Who are you?" he demands.

"I'm sorry. I think I'm in the wrong spot. I should go." I point toward the door and move in that direction, but he cuts me off and traps me at the bookcase again.

"I don't think so. What are you doing here?" he questions.

"I'm... I was just lost, and the door was open." I should have thought of a good cover story in case this situation occurred.

"This part of the building is off-limits to the auction girls. You're supposed to be downstairs already. How did you get back here?" He continues with his questions.

"Auction girls?" I glance down at my attire. Black slacks and a long-sleeved black blouse don't exactly scream sexy, but the way he's talking, that's what he's looking for.

He looks at the box in his hands, turning it one way, then the other. Probably to see if I've broken it when I dropped it.

"Look. I was just looking around. No big deal. Just let me go." I make like I'm going to move past him. He blocks me again.

"You'll need to wait here."

"Wait? For what?" I can't wait. I don't want to wait. I want to get out of here. Too much is at risk if I stay here.

"Me. You're waiting for me." a dark voice thunders from the doorway.

TWO

MEGAN

Ice dances up my spine before I set eyes on him, and once I do, my insides freeze completely over.

Alexander Volkov stands in the doorway. His dark-brown eyes fix on me, pinning me to the floor with his cold glare. The same look he had in in the antechamber, only darker now that it's settled completely on me.

I swallow back the little cry trying to escape and roll my shoulders back.

Alexander Volkov owns Obsidian, a not-so-secret secret club that caters to pretty much anything and everyone who lives outside the lines of the law. He and his brothers also own a small handful of other clubs in the city. Those are the legal businesses that give him creditability with high society. He and his family show up at high-profile events, making their way into the society papers.

His picture has made its way into the newsreels more than once over speculations of his unsavory business dealings. He has the sort of face that makes you stop scrolling when you see it. Strong jaw, neatly trimmed beard, but it's the eyes.

The deep-set dark gaze that traps you even through a photograph.

But now his cold eyes are focused on me—in person—and my nerves are back on edge.

Okay. I can get out of this.

So what that no one knows I'm here.

I haven't told anyone what I'm up to.

And the one person who would notice right away that I've gone missing is already missing in action.

That's okay. I can still figure this out. I just need a second.

I'm sure I'll be able to just walk right out of this place without any further issues. I just need to explain why I'm here.

"I'm sorry." My voice holds firm. Good. Good start, Megan. "I was looking for the bathroom…" I try to throw on a flirtatious smile, but his eyebrow peaking into a sharp arch over his left eye suggests I missed the mark.

"She had this." My captor hands the box with the name Dexter Thompson etched into the side over to Alexander.

He looks at the name, runs his thick fingers over it, then brings his eyes up to me again. His jaw tightens.

"Go." He jerks his head to the door and the man who found me hurries from the room, pulling the door closed behind him.

"Look, I know—"

"Who are you?" he cuts me off.

"Me? I'm no one." Again, I try to laugh off the danger I'm in. "Just lost is all. If you'll just point me in the direction to the exit, I'll be on my way."

His stoic expression gives me pause. Do I just walk out of here, or should I wait for him to say something?

I decide to start moving toward the door. He doesn't stop me, so I take it as a good sign, hurrying my steps to the exit.

"Your name," he orders when I get one step from the door.

"You're wearing one of our uniforms, but there's no name tag. What's your name?"

My hand is on the handle. A name tag. Damn. I've made a complete mess of this whole thing.

"It doesn't matter. But thanks for... well, thanks." I push the wrought iron rolled handle down, expecting the door to open for me. It doesn't.

"It's locked," he says casually from behind me. My heart leaps into a run and I pull again and again, each time pushing the handle down harder and yanking harder.

His sigh could part the sea.

I give up and flip around, pushing my back against the thick wooden door. I'm trapped in this room. In this secret room in the secret part of this secret building with a man who has no reputation for mercy or kindness.

His eyebrows lift. "Your name."

I swallow hard around the bundle of nerves taking my voice box hostage.

"Megan," I finally push out.

"Megan what?" he presses.

"Why do you need my full name?" I question, my throat constricting around my words as they work their way out.

His stare makes my skin heat, and it's getting worse the longer he keeps it on me. I have a sense that he's not going to explain himself. He's going to just outwait me.

"Reed. Megan Reed." No sense in lying at this point. I'm stuck here and I'm sure there's a whole room in this place dedicated to getting people to spill their secrets.

The Volkov family isn't exactly in the business of showing mercy to its enemies. He may look all businesslike walking around in that insanely expensive-looking suit and posing for the cameras at influential events, but it's not a huge secret what the Volkov family really is.

Mafia.

"What are you doing here in my office, Megan Reed?" He flips the lid on the box in his hands. "What would you want with this?"

I really should have had a more thorough plan before I decided to put my life on the line for this little adventure.

"With the box?" Stalling might get me a few more moments, but eventually I have to answer. The truth is out. No way I'm giving him that. Not if I want this little adventure to be a success.

And I want—no, desperately need—this to go my way.

"Yes, Megan Reed. What do you want with this box? Why are you in this office?"

"Like I said, I got lost. I was just looking for another bathroom." It could happen, I suppose.

It's plausible.

"You got lost?"

"Yes." I nod to emphasize my answer. "I was just looking for the women's room. That's... that's all." I swallow, saying a silent prayer that he'll believe me.

"The bathroom." He shakes his head. "You should try telling the truth, Megan Reed. The waitstaff used on the upper floor of the club aren't allowed past the antechamber. You're not wearing a name tag or the right uniform that would suggest you're working on the lower level tonight. And there are at least three restrooms available to staff before entering this part of the building. So, Megan Reed. I'll give you another shot. Why are you in my office?"

My brain races. I'm never good when put on the spot like this. Even when I had the answer, if a teacher called on me in class, I would freeze. I'm not one for the spotlight.

"It's uh... just a prank." I wince internally. Who would be stupid enough to pull a prank on this place? The Volkov family may host charity events and pretend to be just any other elitist family, but there's enough rumors about what happens to people who go against them for me to understand being here is dangerous.

And yet I'm here.

"A prank?" He snaps the lid shut.

"Yes." I shove off the door. "Hazing."

Okay, yeah, this could work. The school year just started.

"For Greek Week." Is that what they call it? The junior college I went to didn't exactly have sororities.

"Hazing for what?" He continues his questions. I can't tell if he believes me or not. His thoughts are well guarded behind his cold exterior. Even his jaw has sharp edges.

"Uh... Delta... Omega... Phi?" I clear my throat, hoping to hide the little question at the end of the name. It sounds legit, but I have no idea if the university actually has such a sorority.

"Delta Omega Phi." He arches a brow. "And what did they want you to do? Steal this box? Why this one?" He twists slightly and drops the box on the desk behind him.

"Look." I try to loosen my stance. "I have no idea. This is a prank that's gone terribly wrong. So, if you'll just let me go, I'll get back."

"Who runs the Delta Omega Phi?" he asks casually.

I laugh. It's forced and fake and even I know I'm blowing this, but still, I forge on.

"I can't tell you that. It's part of the whole hazing thing." I'm horrible at this. I never should have thought I'd get away with it.

I should have stuck with the bathroom story.

"How did you know where this room was? How did you get into this part of the building?" His questions shoot off in rapid fire with each step he takes toward me.

"Um, I don't know." I lower my chin, trying to glare at him. "They just told me."

"Who is they?" He's in front of me now. The tips of his polished, too expensive shoes nearly touching me.

"I can't say." I have to lean my head back to look at him.

"Won't say, because you can." He pauses only a beat.

"What?" I flick my gaze to the windows.

Maybe I can get one open and get outside before he grabs me. But even if I do, can I get across the vast lawn and out the front gate before his men tackle me to the ground? Or worse, put a bullet in me. Mira might find out I was dead and come running back straight into the hands of a bigger monster.

No. I have to get out of here free and clear.

His eyes harden when I keep silent. In half a breath, he's on me, one heavy hand around my throat.

"When I ask you something, it's best to answer the first time." His fingers tighten around my throat while he surveys my face. Using both hands, I yank on his wrists, but he's not budging.

"Let me go," I say, still trying to get out of his grasp.

"Megan." He says my name softly, like he's playing with it.

"Yeah. I already said that." I slap his wrists. "Let go."

He presses his body against mine. Hard and unyielding, the man is made of the same stone the rest of the place is.

His eyes wander over my hair. With his free hand, he picks up a lock of it and rubs it between his fingers.

"I've seen highlights before, but this is... pure white." He tilts his head to look at the rest of my hair, at the other streaks of white.

It's not a dye job, but I'm more concerned with getting his hand off my throat than explaining it to him.

"Let go," I urge again.

He drops my hair and brings his dark eyes back to mine.

"How did you get this uniform?" He flicks the lapel of the black vest.

"From the storage room. I came in with the other staff."

His eyes narrow. "Identification is checked at the staff entrance."

I nod. "Yeah, there was a guy there, but he got a phone call and just waved us in." I had thanked the stars and the moon for that bit of luck, but it seems my luck has run out.

He drops his hand from my throat and pulls a phone from the inside pocket of his suit jacket. With his eyes locked on me, he presses the phone to his ear.

"Send Igor to me," he orders, then hangs up.

"This was obviously a huge mistake and I'm sorry if I messed up your night. It sounds like you have a lot going on. You can just let me go." I grab the handle and shove it downward, but it's still locked.

He moves to the desk and leans back against it, folding his arms over his chest. Moments tick by, and I continue to rack my brain for a way out of this room and this building. The entire time he watches me, as though he's trying to figure me out.

Well, good luck to him, because I haven't recognized myself in months.

There's a knock on the door behind me, breaking the silence of the room. Alexander steps up to me, waiting for me to stand aside before reaching for the door. He slides the plate of the handle to the left before turning it downward. It opens up.

"Come inside." He pulls the door open enough for Igor to step in and shuts it before I can move a single muscle toward it.

"You needed something?" Igor's a rough-looking man.

A jagged scar runs across his neck, like someone tried slitting his throat once. His hair is shaved short, showing two more scars on his scalp.

"You were in charge of security at the employee entrance tonight," Alexander states as a matter of fact.

Igor glances my way, his jaw tightening. Word must have spread already about my appearance in the office.

"I was." He rolls his shoulders back, bracing himself.

"You checked every badge?" Alexander's face is emotionless.

Igor's Adam's apple bobs as he swallows hard. "I got a call. I missed a few."

The conversation switches to Russian. Alexander's tone never wavers. Igor's jaw tightens even more and by the end of the conversation, he gives a hard nod and agrees to whatever Alexander is saying.

"Make your offer," Alexander states.

Igor lifts his left arm, offering his hand to Alexander. My mouth dries when I realize his pinky finger is missing the tip. What the hell is happening here?

"What are you doing?" I try to get my feet to move, but I'm glued to the floor by my own fear.

Alexander ignores my question as he grasps Igor's hand, bending it at the wrist until his fingers are all pointed upward. Holding the hand with one hand, he grasps Igor's pinky just above the second knuckle with his other. Muttering something in Russian, Alexander twists the finger while shoving it backward away from the joint at the same time.

A snap crackles the air just before Igor lets out a tortured groan. His finger is bent in the wrong direction at the second knuckle.

My stomach rolls.

Alexander snaps an order, and Igor covers his broken finger with his other hand and nods. Without another word, he opens the door and exits, his face pale as he cradles his broken finger against his chest.

"Why did you do that?" I shout. "You didn't have to do that!"

Alexander shuts the door, sliding the lock back in place before standing toe to toe with me again.

"You are going to tell me exactly why you came to this room and you're going to do it now."

My skin electrifies with him so close. It intensifies tenfold when he wraps his huge hand around my throat again.

"And if I don't? Are you going to break my finger too?" With one squeeze, he can snuff me out.

But if I tell him what he wants to know, I might not be able to pull this off again, and I still need to get to the rest of the things in that box.

He lowers his mouth to my ear, nipping my earlobe.

"If you don't tell me, I'll rip off those pants, bend you over that desk, and make you wish you had."

Three

Alexander

Megan Reed is no sorority-rushing college student. The woman standing before me now, beneath my grip, glaring icy-blue eyes up at me, holds no resemblance to some wide-eyed freshman.

She's nervous, though. Witnessing Igor's punishment for his failure has affected her. The pulse in her neck is racing.

Part of me wants to run my tongue over that vein. To inhale her fear.

She's right to be afraid. Men who have trespassed here haven't been treated as well as she has been so far. I wonder how long she'd hold up against the terrible things I could do to her.

The horrific things I want to do to her. How pretty is she when she cries?

Fuck, I'm a monster. I want to hear all the different little whimpers she can give me.

"Just let me go." Her words sneak past her lips. There are no tears yet.

Pity.

"If this is just a prank, tell me who sent you, and how did they know how to get to this office?" I keep slight pressure on her throat while I continue my questioning.

She had looked so damn proud of herself when she'd exited the antechamber. While this part of the building is kept hidden from the prying eyes of the outside world, everything that happens in here can be watched on the CCTV system we have set up.

I noticed her right away in the antechamber. Our staff is required to have a severely polished look that blends into the background. Megan stood out immediately with those white stripes in her hair. If she were truly a member of our serving crew, she'd have been made to dye her hair.

But it was the tinge of fear in her eyes that completely gave her away. She tried to hide out in the open, and when that didn't work, she wove herself through the room, trying to stay behind anyone who might block her presence.

But this is my club, and nothing happens here that I don't know about.

Her pulse beats against my fingers as I tighten my grip when her silence continues.

"Don't." She tugs on my wrist.

"Then talk." I run my nose against her cheek. "Unless you want me to throw you over that desk?"

"I don't know. I mean, it wasn't hard to find. It's just an office."

"It wasn't hard to find?" I chuckle.

She had to pass through the central foyer, giving her several options to turn down. One would have led her straight down to the lower level. Another would have led her to the private suites. But she chose, with little hesitation, the hallway leading straight to my door.

"Lying gets you more trouble, Megan. Try again."

"They showed me a picture," she manages, squeezing her eyes shut when I push harder against her throat. I won't cut off her air, but she doesn't know that. It's better she keeps guessing how far I'm capable of going.

There's a reason this place is kept out of the prying eyes of the outside world. Men go to great lengths to keep our secrets ours. If there's a crack in the foundation, I need to know about it now.

The secrecy of this place makes this part of my business sought after. Men like to think they're part of something bigger, something more elite than those they feel are beneath them.

"What picture?" I lessen my grip.

Her throat works beneath my hand.

"Get off me!" She thrusts both hands at my chest and drives up her knee at my groin. Silly girl, everything she does plays out in those clear eyes first.

I easily evade her knee, and her shove does nothing but irritate me further.

"Fine," I grind out. "You want to play this your way; we'll do it your way." Releasing her throat, I move my grip to her hair, fisting the dark and white locks at the roots.

She cries out as I drag her across the room.

I shove her over the edge of the desk, pushing her farther up until her toes barely touch the floor.

"Stop!" she screams, writhing on the desk, trying to scramble away, but I still have her hair. She's going nowhere.

With my free hand, I grab the elastic band of her slacks and yank them down with such force, they tear a little at the hip.

"No!" She wiggles faster, kicking her legs out.

Dragging her more toward the edge, her ass is exactly where I want it.

"You had your chance." I bring my hand down across her pale skin, giving no mercy.

"No!" She tries to twist, but again, I have her hair. She's going to have to give it over soon.

Another swat and another, again and again I spank her generous ass until red blotches cover her skin. It's a beautiful sight, and I take a moment to appreciate it.

"Okay! Okay!" Her legs still. "I'll tell you!"

"I know you will." I acknowledge, spreading more smacks across her ass, lowering my aim until I'm nearing her thighs. "When I'm done, you'll tell me everything."

"Stop. Please." Her voice softens, but I'm not done yet.

"I gave you a chance to do this easy. You wanted this." I slap her ass harder. The dim lighting of the room is just enough for me to make out the redness darkening.

She's slack over the desk. Her toes scrape across the Moroccan rug my brother brought back from one of his more adventurous excursions.

Slowly, I run my hand over her heated skin. Not soothing her, but to memorize the feel of her.

"Tell me," I say, loosening my grip in her hair.

"Let me up," she demands softly. Even with her ass freshly spanked, she still has steel in her voice.

I grin down at her. There's no harm, she can't see me.

"Better you stay in position, just in case we need to revisit." I pat her ass just enough to enjoy the bounce of her cheek.

Fuck, this is getting uncomfortable. My cock lengthens, pressing against the zipper of my slacks.

"So talk." I lean my hip against the desk.

"Fine. I wasn't given any information. Only told to get inside and bring back some token. That's all. I found your office by mistake." She sniffles.

I press my hand against her bare ass. "Lucky you. How'd you know there was an event tonight?"

We don't employ waitstaff every night, only during special events.

"Lucky guess." It's more of a question than an answer.

If someone gave her the layout of the club, I need to know who it is. Even more so if they were aware of the auction tonight.

"Who gave you the information?" I ask.

"I swear. No one. I... I saw someone go in the service entrance and I figured I'd try that way. Really. Just a lucky guess." There's a hesitation in her voice.

She's obviously covering up for whoever actually sent her here. No one has that much luck to show up on an auction night, get past security and find an unused uniform, then magically locate my office and just happen to find the vault behind the books. But whoever she's protecting must frighten her more than me, or she's extremely good at playing the naive girl.

"You can get up." I step away from her, watching as she slides off the desk. Her hair falls over her face as she works her pants and panties back up over her hips.

"You're an asshole." She turns her fiery eyes on me.

Watching a grown man get his finger broken must not have affected her the way I thought it would. She seems to have forgotten all about it already.

"You're stubborn. You could have told me that at the start and avoided this." I fold my arms over my chest. "Unless there's more to it?"

I narrow my gaze, watching her expression. Liars have tells. I just need to find hers.

"No." She shakes her hair out of her face, wiping away a

strand that gets stuck in a tear track. Again, I wonder how sweet her tears must taste.

"Then why not just come clean?"

Her gaze slides to the book on the desk, just out of her reach.

"I need something to take back."

Brave, stubborn girl.

"No." I pick up the book. "You can go back empty-handed."

I'm still not buying the sorority bullshit, but if she wants to keep up the pretense, fine. She didn't get anything, and the auction downstairs is going to be starting soon.

"I can't." Her jaw tightens.

I glance at the box she had in her hands when she was caught. Why that box?

"How do you know Dexter Thompson? Do you work for him?"

"I don't know him. Like I said, I just needed something, anything."

"So, you found the cabinet hidden behind the books... You could have just taken something from the desk," I point out.

"I... I was pulling a book out when the thing opened. I was just being curious when I grabbed the box."

I arch an eyebrow.

"You know what happened to the kitten who got too curious."

She pales. "It was just a prank."

"Prank's over, then," I say firmly. "If I ever see you here again, though, Megan Reed, understand things will be much worse for you than just a little hand spanking."

She raises her chin.

"Not even a stapler?"

She maintains her glare, even with her eyes still shimmering from the tears spilling from the spanking I gave her. There's still fear in her eyes, but she's pushing through it. Determined to get what she came for.

Impressive.

"Show them my handprints on your ass." I pull my phone out from my inside pocket of my suit jacket, tapping out an order for a car to be brought to the back entrance of the wing.

I grab her elbow and half drag her to the door. Just touching her makes me want to throw her over the desk again. Not to spank her this time, but to find out if her pussy is as wet as my dick is hard.

She tries to tug out of my grasp as I pull her down the corridor, but she's no match for my strength.

Harold waits for me in the foyer when we exit the corridor through a proper door.

"Is the car ready?" I ask.

"Yes." His gaze quickly flickers to her but returns to me immediately.

A thunderous bout of clapping comes from down the staircase, and she turns to look.

"What's going on down there?" she questions, keeping up with me but barely. "The other guy said there was an auction. What is that?"

I grit my teeth.

"Nothing you need to concern yourself with. You're going home." I throw open the back door and get her down the stairs to the waiting car without letting her fall on her face.

The driver has the back door open when we approach.

"Get in."

"I have my own car." She tries to get loose again.

"It will be dropped off. Get in." I jerk my chin to the car. "Unless you need more convincing that doing what I say the first time I say is the best course of action? Maybe Igor can clarify things for you?"

She purses her lips together.

"Get in." I put three fingers up in the air. "You have three seconds, and then Dominic here is going to have some entertainment."

Her cheeks flush.

"Fuck you." She climbs into the car. "You don't even know which car is mine—" I slam the door on her words.

"Take her home and make sure she goes inside," I instruct Dominic. "Then park and get comfortable. I want eyes on her tonight. If she leaves, you follow. If anyone shows up, I want you to find out who it is. Understand?"

If she was trying to get information for someone, they'll most likely try to contact her tonight. Or she'll try to meet with them.

"You got it, boss." He tips his head, then hurries around the car to get inside.

Megan Reed glares out the window at me as the car pulls away. Once the car makes its way down the alley, I turn to head back inside.

Yuri runs down the steps, worry wrinkling his expression.

"Is she gone?" He stares down the drive.

"What's wrong?"

"I checked the box before I put it back. The drive is gone." He shoves his hand through his hair.

"What drive?" My teeth snap as I clench my jaw.

"The little flash drive with everything we had on Dexter Thompson. It's gone."

She gave in so easily. Went into the car with such little fight.

I thought she'd finally learned her lesson.

Staring down the drive with him, I clench my hands. "Not a problem. I'll get it back."

Four

Megan

My eyes fly open at the sound of footsteps in my bedroom. Paralysis kicks in, and I'm frozen beneath the flat sheet.

I wait for another sound.

Nothing.

Slowly, I start breathing again, my muscles loosen, and I roll over to my back.

The fan on my dresser blows the sheet against my skin as I lie still, listening for any other noises.

Letting out a long breath, I convince myself it was nothing. Maybe the neighbors upstairs dropped something. A noise from the street outside. It could be anything.

Not every bump in the night means the DeAngelos' enforcer is crawling through my window with his Glock and silencer aimed at my head. It could just as easily be a cat.

Relaxing back into my pillows, I try to force myself back to sleep. This whole thing is going to be over in a few days.

Once I hand over that drive, this whole nightmare will be

over. Instead of fear and paranoia, I'll be able to go back to eating ramen noodles and Rice-A-Roni for dinner.

Mira can come home.

It's going to be fine.

Footsteps sound.

They're definitely footsteps.

In the living room?

No, not in the apartment.

Please, not in the apartment.

Before I freeze up again, I slide out from beneath the sheet. I grab the knife I keep in the top drawer of my nightstand, right next to my vibrator, and pad across the room.

The door's halfway open, so I can get a good view down the hall to the living room.

Absolute darkness.

Hyping myself up with deep breaths, I gear up for going out there.

Another footstep.

Or did a window close?

Using my bare foot, I nudge the door open enough for me to slide through. Mira's bedroom door is still shut and across the hall, the bathroom door is closed. But did I shut it before I went to bed?

All this fear is muddling up my memory.

Slowly, I tiptoe down the hall. Each step makes my palm holding the knife sweat.

"Is someone there?" I call out, wincing at my own stupidity. If there is someone there, they're not going to just announce themselves.

Yet I still wait a moment.

"Mira?" My voice wavers.

Nothing.

I haven't heard from her in over a month; the possibility

that she's shown up in the middle of the night is pretty damn slim.

Once at the end of the hall, I lean toward the living room, trying to take a peek around the space. It's quiet. The oscillating fan in the corner of the room blows the papers on the coffee table, rustling them. Could that be what I was hearing?

I step into the room.

Empty.

The kitchen is just off the living room. It only takes a few steps into the room to be able to see it's empty as well.

I drop my hand to my side with a sigh. The stress is going to send me to an early grave if this keeps up.

Checking the front door once more to make sure it's locked, I head back to my bed. There's still time. Marco wouldn't send anyone yet. He gave me another week.

If I don't make this trade, though, then I'll be having more than nightmares about what will happen to me.

Shoving my bedroom door open, a dark figure comes into view.

"Megan." His voice rattles me. He's standing in front of the window, shrouding his face in shadow.

I'm frozen again.

The knife!

With jerky movements, I raise my right hand with the knife, like I'm in a slasher movie and I'm going to end the monster terrifying the village.

"You're going to hurt yourself with that." He leans down and flicks on the little lamp on my nightstand.

Yellow lighting hits Alexander's face as he stands to his full height.

"Put it down." He nudges his chin toward the dresser next to me.

I look behind me, then at the bathroom door; it's still closed.

"Where did you come from?" The living room had been empty. He would have had to pass me if he came from that direction to get into my bedroom.

"The knife, Megan." He points a leather-covered finger at me. He's covered in black from shoulder to toe.

No fingerprints left behind.

My throat swells.

"How did you get in here?" I ask, waving the knife again.

He sighs.

"I got lucky and came across your door." The snark and the annoyance mingle together perfectly in his tone as he throws my own bullshit back at me.

He gives a pointed look at my hand. "Put it down or I'll take it. And if I have to do that, it gets added to the list."

"What list? Why are you here?" I ask, instead of doing what he says. He's in my house uninvited, and I'm the one holding the knife. I don't think he understands who has the upper hand here.

"Stubborn girl." He's at me in two long strides and before I can even blink, my wrist twists, pain shoots up my forearm, and the knife is gone.

"Ow!" I grab hold of my wrist and cradle it against me.

He has my knife and is inspecting it while frowning.

"This thing is useless." He bends the tip of it with his thumb, then lets go. It probably is. I've never actually tried to use it before, and I got it from the secondhand store because it looked scary.

"What do you want?" I ask, moving back a step.

"You took something that belongs to me." He slides over with me, staying right in front of me, giving me no room to run. "I want it back."

Of course, he'd want it back, but I can't give it to him. No matter what he threatens, it has to stay with me. I can't keep Mira safe if he takes it.

"I did not. You took the box back." I swallow around my lie as I tilt my head back to look into his dark eyes. His brow wrinkles with more annoyance.

"More lies." His voice dips.

"I... what do you think I took? If you describe it, maybe I can tell you if I saw it." I reach back like I'm going to lean against the dresser.

There's almost always something littering the top of my dresser, a plate from a late-night snack, an old coffee mug, anything that might give a little weight that I can hit him over the head with.

He leans into me, bracing himself on the edge of the dresser at the same time as covering my hands with his.

"I'm not playing games with you. I've wasted enough time on you tonight. Give me back what you took and maybe you'll have a chance at sitting sometime next week." The threat, which definitely sounds closer to a vow, washes over me.

Between the growly way he says it, the smell of his aftershave, and the sexy way his eyes wrinkle as they bore into me, my insides catch fire.

Not the response he was looking for, I'm sure.

"I... I can't," I manage to get out, while trying to worm my hands out from beneath his. "Really. I can't."

"Why is that?" He lowers his face closer to mine. "Why can't you give me what you stole? You haven't given it to anyone yet. You haven't left your apartment since you arrived home. And no one has been here to see you, so what excuse do you have?"

My throat dries.

Telling him won't matter. He doesn't exactly give off the

hero vibe. There's little chance that he'd climb a white horse and go off into battle with Marco DeAngelo to get me out of my mess.

"Please."

His eyebrow arches.

"You really want to do this the hard way again, Megan?"

"No." I shake my head, remembering how hard his hand was earlier. "I don't want to do this any way."

The left side of his mouth kicks up just a little, but it falls right back down again.

"I'm sure you don't." He stands up, letting my hands free. "But what you want isn't my concern. You can either give it to me, or I'll just have to find it myself."

He looks around the room, where my unwashed laundry is piled up in front of the closet, and my washed, but unfolded laundry overflows my only laundry basket next to the mountain.

He yanks open the top dresser drawer, hitting my hip with the corner as he does so. I stare, dumbstruck, as he rifles through my panties and my socks.

"Hmm." He lifts a pair of black lace panties I'd bought while dating Jerad, my ex-boyfriend, in hopes of getting his attention away from the video games he loved so much.

I snatch them from his fingers.

"I want you to leave." There.

He huffs a laugh and shuts the dresser.

"I already told you what I thought about what you want." He moves through my room, his booted feet making no sound against the ugly blue carpeting.

He yanks open the nightstand drawer where my knife came from.

Where my vibrator lives.

Mortification will kill me tonight, and I would deserve it.

"Just stop."

He picks up the bullet and cocks an eyebrow as he brings it to his nose. Inhaling, his mouth spreads open into a knowing grin.

"I guess our meeting earlier left a bigger impression on you than I thought." He drops the tattletale of a toy back into the drawer. I knew I should have gotten up right away to wash it instead of waiting until morning.

"I haven't given you a second thought since I was dropped off," I lie. He's been all over my thoughts since I was driven away from Pulse.

"Another lie." He shakes his head. "You know, it's getting long."

"What is?" I fold my arms over my chest. His eyes roam over me, lingering on my thighs. My positioning has raised my sleep shirt up, showing off the entire length of my legs.

"The list of reasons to punish you." He rifles through the second drawer, ignoring the notepad and pens there, then goes to my closet.

"You're wasting your time." I stomp over to the closet and shove the door shut before he can get his hands on any of the hangers. It's not even in there, but I'm not letting him go through my clothes so he can judge me.

"You really want to play that game?" His eyes narrow. "Because if we play it, you're going to lose, and when you lose, I'm really going to enjoy the prize."

My skin electrifies beneath his words. It's like he's threatening me and promising me all at the same time and it has completely confused my body.

"I'm not playing games. You need to leave." I jerk my hand at the door.

His gaze skims over me, then follows my arm to the open bedroom door. A devious smile tugs on his lips.

"All right, Megan Reed. We'll play your little game." He steps closer to me, the toes of his boots resting just beside my bare toes on the carpet. "I will take five minutes. And if I find what I'm looking for, you lose. And if I can't find it, I'll leave."

"Five minutes?" He'll never find it, I'm sure of it. "And then you'll leave?"

"You don't want to know what my prize is if I win?" He tilts his head a little to the right.

"You're not going to win, but sure, what's your prize?"

"I get to see you on your hands and knees, naked, begging for a mercy I won't grant. Because." He runs the back of his leather-covered fingers along my jaw. "My prize is your tears."

He's a madman.

A rich, insanely handsome madman, but still, he's completely off his rocker.

"Five minutes." I barely get my voice to work. "Starting now." I glance at the clock on my nightstand. Two fifteen.

He steps around me, walks out of the bedroom, and down the hall. I follow him, my heart racing right along with me.

Through the living room, then to the kitchen.

I stop in front of my couch.

He can't possibly know.

How can he?

He'd been searching my bedroom, and then he just all of a sudden goes to the kitchen?

He's playing with me.

He is fucking with me.

He opens the freezer, takes out the open bag of peas, reaches inside, and pulls out the little flash drive.

The flash drive I stole from the Volkov family.

The flash drive I need to exchange to save Mira's life so she can stop hiding and come home.

"Look here, Megan." He smiles. "I win."

Five

Alexander

Fuck, she's gorgeous when she's afraid.

I know it makes me a monster to think it, and an even bigger one for getting so fucking hard when her eyes widen like this. Her mouth drops open, and I can practically smell the panic rolling off her.

"You don't know that's yours," she tries to deny me my victory.

I drop the bag of peas back into the freezer and shut the door, pocketing the drive to keep it safe.

"My car dropped you off at ten fourteen." I move in her direction. "I've had four hours to find out everything I need to know about you, Megan Reed. Twenty-five-year-old administrative assistant to Carl Swinkler at Cinders Industries. Not some little college girl rushing Delta Omega Phi, a sorority that doesn't exist."

Her throat works when she swallows hard as I get closer to her. The nightshirt she's wearing is too big. The neckline dips enough in the front; the swell of her breasts show.

"Oh." The word pops out so softly, I'm not sure she meant it to.

"After you went to sleep two hours ago, it gave me plenty of time to search your apartment. I even had time to watch you sleep. Do you know you grind your teeth? You should probably wear some sort of mouth guard for that."

Her cheeks flush, just a little. A dusting of pink brushes her cheeks, enough for me to know she's thinking about what else I might have seen while I was lurking in the shadows.

I'd been too late for her playtime with the bullet vibe in her nightstand, but she can keep wondering if I was here or not.

"I'm going to give you a chance to tell me why you wanted the drive. And then I'm going to take you back to your bedroom, put you on your hands and knees, and punish you until you beg me to stop. And then." I stop just in front of her. "I'm going to start all over again."

She blanches.

"I'll scream," she threatens.

"I'm looking forward to it." I nod.

"The people upstairs will hear." She backs up a step. Catching her in this shoebox of an apartment won't be hard.

"They're on vacation," I say with a tilt to my head. "Don't you talk to your neighbors? The drunk across the hall is probably passed out by now. And I doubt any of the other people in the building will care if they hear you."

This entire building is probably on some FBI watch list. The criminals that live here won't lift a finger to help her, and the other tenants are smart enough to stay out of business that isn't theirs.

She can't believe she lives in a safe neighborhood. She sleeps with a dull butcher knife next to her vibrator.

She should have a better weapon. Something with actual

power behind it that she can utilize without getting close to the attacker.

"So, here's your chance, Megan." I like saying her name. It feels good on my tongue. "Tell me why you wanted the drive."

"It must be really important for you to be here in the middle of the night." She retreats another step, then another, until the back of her legs hit the couch.

"Why did you come looking for the drive on Dexter Thompson? How do you know him?" I advance on her, soaking in the way her pupils dilate as I get closer.

Those pretty blue eyes of hers flick to the right, looking for a way of escape.

Fuck me, I hope she runs.

"You're going to tell me all of your little secrets, Megan Reed." I capture her face in one hand, pinching her cheeks inward until I feel her teeth through her flesh.

The leather makes it harder to get a feel of her skin, but her eyes tell me everything when they go wide. Her pupils all but eviscerate her blue irises.

"I don't have any secrets." Her words squeeze out from my grip.

"Such a little liar." I lower my face to hers, inhaling the sweetness that she is. "Don't worry, I know how to deal with little liars like you."

With my free hand, I unbuckle my belt and yank it from my pants.

Her entire body goes stiff.

"I was going to put you on your knees, but I think this couch will do fine." Releasing her face, I spin her around and push her over the back to the couch.

She's short, so her feet barely touch the hard wood of the floor. For such a shitty building, the floors in the main rooms are actually nice.

As soon as her face hits the cushion, she screams.

She wiggles her arms in front of her and tries to shove off the couch, but there's no escape for her. Not now.

"You had your chance." I push up her nightshirt and find she's wearing a pair of white cotton panties. She's changed out of the black pair she wore earlier.

If her innocence shines through anymore, I might mess my own fucking pants.

"Stop! Stop!" she yells as I pull the elastic of her panties upward until they bunch between her ass cheeks. A wedgie never feels good but couple it with a belting and it's really going to piss her off.

I take a moment to lean over her body, making sure to press my erection against her ass so she knows how happy her discomfort is making me.

"I told you, no mercy," I whisper in her ear.

"Please. Don't." She tries again to get up, but I fist her hair and shove her farther into the couch cushion. Her screams are soaked into the foam of the cushions.

I manage to double over my belt and tuck the buckle into my palm, then take aim at her pretty ass.

She howls after the first lash, kicks and cries as I continue to lash her ass until even in the dimness of the room, I can make out the markings being left by the thick leather.

"Little liar," I mutter as I bring my belt down on her thighs.

She kicks her legs out, but it's no matter. This isn't my first session with a naughty girl.

Her shoulders shake and her sobs are soft when I finally stop the punishment. Laying the belt across her back, I move my attention to her panties.

Using the tip of my middle finger, I run it along the seam of her ass, then farther down. Following the material of her panties, I slide between her thighs, to where her panties have become soaked with her arousal.

She moans, but I can't tell if it's due to embarrassment or her libido. And there's a difference. A woman's humiliation can be as much of an aphrodisiac as any little blue pill.

"You've soaked your panties." I try to sound admonishing, but I'm not at all upset.

I trail my finger farther down until I find her clit, hard and eager to be touched.

This time, her moan is all arousal.

"Not yet. You haven't earned it." I press down on her clit, rubbing it in circles until I'm sure she's starting to ignore the pain in her ass for the pleasure of her pussy.

And then I stop.

"Fuck," she groans.

"Do you think you can be honest with me now?" I ask the back of her head. I wait for the little nod, then help her to her feet.

As soon as her feet are on the floor, she spins around and spits at me. I barely manage to dodge the assault. She needs to get better about her attacks if she's going to keep this up.

"You got what you came for. Just leave." She digs the heels of her hands across her cheeks, wiping away tears.

Shame. I didn't get a chance to enjoy them before she wiped them off.

"You're not going to tell me why you took it?"

Game time is over. It's nearly three in the morning and I have shit to do tomorrow. If she's not going to cooperate, I have no other choice.

Her gaze doesn't meet mine. She's looking everywhere else, my chin, my chest, my ear, but she won't meet my gaze.

"I can't." She sounds tired. Like she's had enough of this, too. "You have it back. Just go."

As I stare at her, I notice her nipples pressing against the nightshirt.

If she'd stolen something useless, like an embossing press with the club logo on it, I could walk out right now and ignore this whole thing. I could go home, wrap my hand around my cock, and play this scene over in my head until I unleashed my climax.

But she hadn't.

She stole Dexter Thompson's flash drive.

And that can't be ignored.

My decision made, I give her a curt nod.

No going back now.

For the second time tonight, I spin her around until her back is to me.

"What are you doing?!" She squirms as I pull her arms behind her. With one hand, I hold her wrists together as I work the zip ties out of my back pocket.

"Enough." I jerk her back toward me when she keeps wiggling.

"Ow! No. That hurts!" She tries to wrench her wrists apart, but I have one zip tie already on. I'm sure it does fucking hurt; that plastic is going to cut into her skin if she keeps this fight up.

I put the second one on, then spin her back to face me.

She brings her head back, like she's going to try and head-butt me.

I only sigh, then bend over and throw my shoulder into her stomach.

There's a groan when I have her hoisted up.

"No! No!" She kicks and I wish I had brought the straps for her legs. But I hadn't thought things would get this far.

She should have been scared enough to spill the truth by now.

Carrying her around makes me move a little slower, but I manage to grab a few things, then head out the door, locking it once we're outside.

"Help! Help!" She's doing her best, but really, it's the middle of the night and no one's coming to help her in this place.

She groans more when I jog down the flight of stairs. I parked in front of the building, so it's not a far distance.

The trunk pops as soon as I get close enough.

"Boss?" Yogi steps up to the car.

"I have it from here," I assure him. "But go inside and make sure there's no lingering issues."

"Not a problem."

I dump her into the trunk. Thankfully, she's too stunned at first to do much other than shake her hair away from her face.

I don't have any more time to spend on her yelling and threats, so I start to close the trunk.

"Wait!"

I pause. She looks surprised, like she didn't think it would work.

"You had your chance, Megan. Remember that. I gave you every chance."

"Please!"

The trunk slams on her cry.

Once inside the car, I turn the music on to cover any noise she's making back there.

Pulling away from her shit apartment building, I head back to my part of town.

We have a place for people like her. For those who cross us.

And she's going to hate it.

Six

ALEXANDER

"I heard you had a fun night." My brother, Ivan, takes the seat beside me at the long, oblong stone table.

"I had an eventful night," I say, sliding my phone into the breast pocket of my suit. It's the dozenth time I've checked on my little captive this afternoon.

She has grit, I'll give her that. Not one to take being a prisoner lying down, she's tried everything to get the door open.

After she threw herself into the door, she's going to need her shoulder looked at. The only thing she achieved was being bounced halfway across the room.

It's been a distraction watching her all day.

"Eventful?" He drums his fingertips on the table. "From what I heard, you chased down a woman who had managed to break into Obsidian. In the middle of the night, no less. If you didn't enjoy that, you did it wrong."

"I didn't say I didn't enjoy myself." I could have enjoyed myself more if she would have been cooperative.

I would have shown her how I reward honesty. She would

have been screaming for entirely different reasons if she'd only given over.

"So, what's the big news that we all had to crawl out of bed on a Saturday morning and get in here?" Kaz strolls into the room with a venti coffee and his sunglasses covering his eyes.

"It's two in the afternoon," Ivan says. "Have a good night, then?"

Kaz pulls out a chair and throws himself into it, putting his coffee down and leaning his head back against the headrest.

"Definitely worth it." He grins, sliding his sunglasses off and tossing them on the table. "Now, what's the problem?"

"Our brother here found a girl in his office last night. She stole the flash drive for Dexter Thompson." Ivan brings our youngest brother up to speed.

"Dexter Thompson? Which one's that?" He runs a hand through his short black hair.

"The zoning commissioner," I remind him. "The one who's going to make sure we're able to get all the shit we need to open the casino resort up north. That guy."

Kaz raises his brow. "Why did she want his drive? Is she trying to open a business and needs some dirt on him to make sure everything happens in a timely fashion?"

"No." I sigh. "Can you focus?"

He drinks some of his coffee. "I'm trying, but it's early. Some of us actually enjoy our evenings. It's not all business, business, business."

"Well, if you could bring yourself to focus on business for a little while this afternoon, I'd appreciate it," I say.

He shakes his head.

"Fine. So you caught her. Got it back?"

"Yes."

"Then what's the problem?" He lifts a shoulder.

"The problem is we don't know why she would want the drive in the first place."

"Did you ask her?" He leans forward. "You know, really ask her."

"She's not in the pit if that's what you mean." I shake my head.

"That would get her to answer pretty quick, though." Ivan acknowledges. "What do you know about her so far?"

"Nothing out of the ordinary. She's twenty-five, lives in a shit apartment on the south side with a roommate who is out of town at the moment, and she works at Cinders Industries as an administrative assistant."

"She could be working for someone inside the Cinders organization but on the side. There could still be a tie there somewhere," Ivan says.

"I'm getting the staff list today, but it's a small start-up. I doubt they'd be involved."

"Maybe Dexter finally found his balls and hired her?" Kaz offers, sipping more of his coffee.

"I think she would have given him up if it was him." I shake my head. "Whatever the reason she did it, she's afraid of them."

"More afraid of them than you?" Kaz scoffs. "You should have put her in the pit."

"Where is she now?" Ivan asks.

"I have her." I splay my hands on the table. "I will deal with her."

"In the meantime, we should have all the files in that room moved," Ivan says.

"I already ordered it done. It's all been moved to my place," I explain.

"Where your captive is? You sure that's a good idea?" Kaz leans his forearms on the table.

"It's fine. She doesn't know anything's there, and she wouldn't know where to look. Plus, she's not walking around freely anyway. I'm going to get to the bottom of all of this." I give him a hard look.

I won't be deterred. If she's hiding who is behind her little heist yesterday, I have no doubt it is for a good reason.

She could be in danger.

And from the level of stubbornness she's displayed so far, I doubt she would concede to needing help to get out of whatever trouble she's in.

The girl's a distraction. Yes. An annoyance? Yes.

But she's mine for the time being.

"And if she doesn't give information?" Ivan questions.

I bring my gaze to his.

"She will." Now that she's in my possession, and once I have the time to do as I please, she won't be able to get away without giving it.

"What do you need from us?" Ivan asks.

"There's a charity dinner tonight. Dexter is going to be there. I need one of you to go and keep an eye on him. He could be behind this, or someone else is trying to get the information we have on him for their own benefit."

"The art gala? I was already planning on going, I'll take care of it." Ivan nods.

Kaz looks over his coffee cup at our brother. "You're going to the art gala, willingly?"

Ivan frowns. "Don't worry about what I'm doing; what are you up to?"

"Nothing good." Kaz grins.

"Children. I'm shackled with children." I sigh.

"Could be worse." Kaz shrugs. "If there's nothing else, I left a very naked woman in my bed, and she's going to start getting upset if I'm not back soon to untie her."

"Willingly tied?" Ivan asks.

"More or less." Kaz laughs as he heads to the door. "Oh, I almost forgot. Last night's auction brought in double the revenue than the last one. I'm going to plan for another one before the end of the year."

"That's fine." I wave a hand.

I pull out my phone again, swiping the screen open.

"Is that her?" Ivan glances over my shoulder as he stands from his seat.

She's standing in the middle of the room, her hands on her hips, her face turned away from the camera.

"It is." I close the screen, shoving my chair back so I can stand.

"You're good with me watching Dexter?" he asks as we make our way out of the room and down the wooden steps to the lower level of the manor.

"The man nearly pisses himself when I get near him; it's probably better you do it anyway." I have little worry he's actually involved.

"I'll chat him up and let you know if anything seems off." Ivan slaps my back. "I have to get going, and you have a night of fun ahead of you." He grins.

Standing on the top of the steps of the manor, I pull out my phone again.

I can't help but take another glance.

This time, my little captive isn't facing away from the camera.

She's glaring straight at it.

Seven

Megan

I'm going to break his nose.

I decided to do it while I've been pacing this damn room. Time isn't a concept I can apply here. There's no clock. No windows to show where the sun is in the sky, or if it's even out.

Every moment runs into the next. I'm just on one big damn loop. Even the room is a continual circle. There are no corners, no straight edges, and the door, an arched wooden slab, is locked.

There's no doorknob, just a round wrought iron door pull, but pulling does nothing to move the damn thing. Pushing didn't get me anywhere either. I can't tell if it's bolted shut or if the door is even real.

It could just be a way to make me think I have a way out when there is none. Maybe he just tossed me in here and will never come back. How long does it take for a human to die without food and water?

My bare feet make no sound on the hardwood as I pace.

There's a narrow bed with a thin blanket and a flat pillow. And a bucket, which I'm getting dangerously close to having to use.

I've beaten the door, stomped on the floor, and all I've gotten for my effort is scratches, bruises, and a broken fingernail. When he finally shows his face, I'm going to break his nose with the metal bucket.

There's a rattling at the door, catching me off guard. It's been so silent, the sound echoes in the small chamber.

Grabbing the bucket, I hurry to the wall beside the door. I have the bucket poised over my head, ready for when whoever comes inside. One fast swing, and I might get a good hit.

Keys rattle. A lock slides open, then a creak of the wood as the door shifts and finally opens into the room.

Shutting my eyes and using all the energy I can muster, I bring the bucket down.

I hit nothing, and the bucket flies out of my hands, clamoring against the floor.

"Megan." His deep sigh tangled with my name sends me into a frenzy. I launch myself at him.

But he easily catches me before I can land a single blow. He shoves me against the wall hard enough to knock the air from my lungs, and just in case that's not enough, he wraps his hand around my throat.

Bringing his forehead against mine, he inhales deeply, then chuckles.

"You have no concept of how much danger you're in, do you?" He raises his eyes, those cold, dark eyes to mine.

There's a thick dusting of a beard along his jaw. The darkness of it contrasts with his perfectly straight white teeth when he grins. There's no pleasure behind it, just more coldness, more sternness.

"I'm already locked in a tower; how much worse can it

get?" I tug on his wrist, but like before, I'm no match for his strength.

"Oh, it can get a lot worse." He reaches down with his free hand, brushing away the hem of my nightshirt, and finds the elastic band of my panties.

"You've been screaming about wanting the bathroom." He pushes on my lower stomach. "Hmmm, full as full can be."

He chuckles, jamming his knee between my thighs when I try to wiggle my legs closed.

Easily, he glides his hand into my panties, over the small patch of short curls, and farther down until the tip of his finger finds my clit.

I close my eyes. Maybe if I shut out the visual, I can ignore the physical.

Except he's not going to let me ignore him.

His finger presses down, running circles over my clit until I'm clenching my teeth.

"I can use this pussy of yours, over and over again, and keep you from ever finding any relief." He slides his hand through my folds, sliding easily through my arousal until he gets to my entrance.

"Stop." I tug on his arm. "Please don't."

Ignoring my plea, he thrusts a finger into me, the heel of his hand putting pressure on my clit now. It's a miracle I keep the moan of pleasure to myself.

It's not my fault.

It's been so long since anyone but me has touched me; my body is just reacting to it. Alexander has nothing to do with it. It's not him.

It's not the spicy aftershave he's wearing. Or the way his eyes seem to see right through me. Or how stern his voice is when he gives a command.

It's a normal anatomical response, and I can't help it.

"Are you going to behave, Megan, so we can talk? Or am I going to have to punish you again? Maybe this time, I'll punish your pussy instead of your ass. Maybe I'll bring you right to the edge and leave you dangling there while I use you."

Arousal twists my insides.

"Or does that turn you on, being used?" He bites down on my earlobe, sending a surge of pleasure straight to the very core of my soul.

"No." I wrench out the word just as he shoves a second finger inside me.

He chuckles.

"It does." He kisses my cheek. "You're no good at lying; you should give it up."

He digs the heel of his palm harder against my clit, and I curl my toes into the wood floor to distract myself. The grip on my throat eases. More air doesn't help me; it only makes me gasp easier as he increases his thrusts with his fingers.

"Show me how good you're going to be for me, Megan," he orders.

It's too hard to listen to him and ignore him. His voice strokes me as easily as his fingers do.

"Don't you dare fucking piss on me." He draws my attention back to another need, but his touch on my clit is overwhelming.

I'm wound tight, a spring that wants to be let loose, and he knows exactly what he's doing. He's not going to let me off this wall until I give him what he wants.

He presses his body against me, my breasts crush against his chest. The warmth of his skin seeps through the black button-down shirt he's wearing. His aftershave fills the space between us.

He bites down on my earlobe again, scraping his teeth over the sensitive spot.

"Be a good girl," he orders, so low, so dark it's almost animalistic.

"Oh. No." I hit at the wall. If I come, will my bladder release too? I'll have to concentrate. I have to hold tight.

"Such a good girl, almost here." He flicks my earlobe with the tip of his tongue, and I imagine it's my clit he's licking. How hard he'd flick it, how wet his tongue would be, how warm his breath would be against my skin.

"No. Oh God!" I bite down on my lip, but it only lasts a moment. As the intensity builds and then blows up within me, my resistance vanishes.

An orgasm rips through my body. Muscles shake, nerve ends rattle, and my soul sighs with relief as the waves of pure pleasure wash over me.

I suck in air, clenching my eyes and pushing my head back against them all. I'm dry; other than my own arousal, I'm dry.

"So fucking responsive." He kisses my cheek again. "Now clean up the mess you made." Before I can focus my eyes on what he's talking about, his fingers shove into my mouth.

Roughly, he drags his fingers over my tongue, cleaning himself of my arousal.

A moment later, he steps away from me, and I have to catch myself before I fall to the floor. He steps back to the door and slams it shut.

The bolt slides into place on the other side, and I realize there was someone out there this entire time. My face burns. Coming like that was humiliating enough. Crying out like I enjoyed it? Even worse. But knowing someone else heard – maybe even witnessed – guts me.

I drag my hand across my mouth then straighten my nightshirt, tugging it down as far as it will go. Not that it matters at this point.

Alexander leans against the door, his arms crossed over his

chest and one foot lazily draped over the other. Needing to get away from him, I scurry across the room, behind the bed.

"I really need to use the restroom," I say after the silence starts to hurt my ears again.

"Then I suggest you answer my questions honestly and quickly. Otherwise, the bucket's still here." He toes the damn thing, and it rolls toward me, clanging as it does so.

"What do you want?" I can plan for his death later. Right now, I need to get him to let me use a real bathroom and then let me go home.

The weekend can't be gone yet, so I should still be able to get home and get to work on Monday. But I don't have the flash drive anymore, so I need to find a new way to make the money I need.

And I only have a few more days for that.

"I want to know the truth. Who sent you to get that flash drive? Was it Dexter Thompson? A member of his staff?" he questions.

"I can't." My shoulders drop. Being kidnapped and tossed into a cell wasn't exactly conducive to getting a good night's sleep. I'm exhausted.

"You can't what?" he presses.

"I can't tell you why or who." The springs in the mattress squeak as I sink onto it. "Because I don't know."

"How can you not know who sent you? You didn't just wake up and decide to sneak into Obsidian and steal Dexter Thompson's information."

"No. I didn't. You're right." I nod, an idea forming in my mind. "I was stepping in for someone while they were on vacation and while I was there, someone slid a piece of paper on the desk I was working at. I just thought it was something for them."

"But it wasn't?"

51

"When I finished what I was doing, I noticed my name was scribbled on the note. It was for me."

"You didn't see the guy who dropped it off?"

"No." I shake my head a little, readjusting my seat to take off some of the pressure from my bladder. "By the time I noticed it was for me, there wasn't anyone else around. The floor was empty."

"And what did it say?"

I squeeze my legs together. "Let me use the bathroom, and I'll tell you."

"Tell me and you can use the restroom. Otherwise." He lowers his gaze at the bucket again.

I hate this man.

"I don't remember exactly. There was a phone number. When I called it, I was given directions for what was needed and the amount I would be paid when I delivered the drive." I speed up my answers. "I have no idea who it was. He used one of those automated voice concealer things. He said directions on where to drop the drive would be delivered if I chose to take the job."

"Why you?"

"I have no idea." I laugh. "It made no sense to me either, but I needed the money." Need it still, but I'm not going into that with him.

"Do you still have the paper?" he asks.

"At home. Yes. You can have it. I don't care. Just let me go." Maybe I can beg Marco to give me more time. Maybe he'll take pity.

He hasn't so far, but desperation is messing with my mind. If it was only my life on the line, maybe I could take the risk. But there's more than me to worry about.

Moments tick by with his dark stare getting more unsettling as it stretches on.

Finally, he shoves off the door and yanks it open.

"There's a bathroom at the end of the hall. There's also a shower, towels, and a change of clothes."

In too great a need for the bathroom to ask any questions, I run from the room, past the guard who undoubtedly heard everything, and head straight for the bathroom.

Once I'm done, when I'm clean and dressed, I'll find a way out of here.

And then a way to fix the mess I've made of my life.

Eight

ALEXANDER

I shouldn't have fucking touched her.

It hadn't been my plan. I was supposed to go in there, threaten her, and make her tell me what I wanted to know.

The fact she hadn't used the washroom since I dumped her in the tower room at my estate was something to be used against her. All it did was probably make her orgasm more intense.

Touching her was reckless. Making her come? That was the real mistake.

She's too relaxed now. Sitting beside me in my car, not in the trunk, but next to me wearing the light-blue sundress one of the housekeepers found for her to wear, distracting me even more with those full fucking thighs on display.

The dress is too fucking short and too tight, but my last attempt at a normal life hadn't left a lot of clothing behind when she walked out. I don't even remember this damn dress. It's something a milkmaid would wear with the rounded neckline pulled tight with a drawstring, and the sleeves have some poof to them.

Even if I could remember the dress, I doubt it looked this good on anyone else. My knuckles whiten as I grip the steering wheel tighter. This isn't a hookup for me to be drooling over. She's a danger. Possibly to my family and definitely to herself.

"You can let me out on the corner. It will be easier than trying to park," she says, tugging at the hem of the dress.

"I'm parking." I pull around the corner from her apartment and find a spot.

"Is my car here?" she asks after I've maneuvered into the spot. "I don't see it on the street."

"Your car had a flat tire. It's being fixed and will be brought over tomorrow night." I throw open my door and climb out. Her door pops open before I round the trunk.

Noticing me glaring at her, she looks down at herself, then back at me. "What's wrong?"

"Nothing." I reach around her and shut the door, hitting my fob to lock it. Though, in this neighborhood, I doubt a car alarm would stop anyone from doing whatever the hell they wanted to it.

"You don't need to walk me up," she says, walking a few paces ahead of me.

I grab hold of her hand, dragging her to my side.

"You're under the delusion that I've set you free, Megan." Turning her to face me once we get to the main door of the building, I wait until she brings her eyes in line with mine. "I haven't. We're just here to get the note."

"But I've told you what you wanted. Look, whatever you and your family do, I don't care. I don't want to know, and I want nothing to do with it."

She's cute, in an incorruptible sort of way.

I wonder how long it would take to ruin that? To rob her of

her innocence and replace it with all the darkness that the world actually holds.

Pulling the door open, I jerk my head. "Let's go."

She rolls her eyes but doesn't argue with me. It's the first smart thing she's done since I put my sights on her at Obsidian.

I follow her inside and up the set of stairs to her apartment. There's a distinct stench of pot lingering in the hall and the music thumping from one of the doors we pass tells me where the party is.

There's a crunch as she steps, and I pull her by the elbow away from whatever she just stepped on.

A glass pipe, or what's left of it after she stepped on the bulbous portion of it, lays splattered on the peeling linoleum tiles.

"Careful." I take the lead, bringing her to the next door, her apartment.

I pull out the key from my pocket.

"Where'd you get that?" She tries to take it from me, but one glance from me and she drops her hand. If she wants to have any chance of getting rid of me after I get this note from her, she needs to behave herself.

I'm not sure she knows how. Which only seems to feed my growing infatuation with her.

As I slip the key into the lock, the door pushes open.

"You didn't have your goon lock it last night?" she accuses, reaching past me to push the door open the rest of the way.

"He locked it." I step in front of her, blocking her from going inside before me.

The living room is trashed. The pillows and cushions are tossed from the couch, and the coffee table is upside down. Picture frames are scattered across the floor from where an end table had been.

"What the hell?" Megan shoves her way into the apartment, but I catch her by the arm before she gets ahead of me.

"Just wait here. Let me make sure there's no one still here." I leave her standing in the living room and quickly check the bedrooms and the bathroom. No one, but the entire place has been gone through.

Drawers are opened, their contents spilled everywhere.

She shuts the front door when I come back from the kitchen. The frame is busted where the bolt had been locked. Whoever got in wasn't trying to be quiet.

The floor trembles from more music pounding from the apartment below.

"I'm going to go out on a limb and say no one heard anything."

She frowns.

"Did your men do this?" she accuses. "Did you send them here to ransack the place while you had me locked up in that house of yours?" Her hands clench at her sides.

"Why would I do that?" I pick up an envelope, a piece of yesterday's mail, turn it over, then toss it back on the counter.

"I don't know." She shoves both hands into her hair, tugging it away from her face. "To get back at me for being able to sneak into your secret fortress?"

"I already punished you for that. No need to do it again." I lift a shoulder and walk past her to the living room. The television, a newer flat-screen model, hasn't been broken. "Nothing seems stolen."

"I have nothing to steal." She picks up the couch cushions and tosses them back onto the couch.

"Where did you have the letter?" I pull us back to the task at hand.

She looks up at me from where she's sitting on the couch, surveying the mess of her apartment.

"The letter?"

"Yes. The letter you got from your secret boss." I gesture toward the bedroom. "Did you hide it somewhere or leave it out?"

"It's in my bedroom. I'll get it." She pushes back up to her feet.

While she's in her room, I head to the kitchen and turn the table back onto its legs. The fridge has a calendar with notes scribbled on the dates when bills are due, a coupon for the pizza place I saw down the street, and a picture of her standing with I assume her parents when she was younger. She's wearing Disney ears and grinning as though she really was standing in the happiest place on earth.

I stand there, mesmerized momentarily by the brightness of her smile. Pure organic happiness that only exists among the innocent shines in her eyes. As much as I loved the little noises she made for me in the tower room, I wonder what she sounds like when pure joy hits her.

No. Not going there. I head to her room when she's been gone for too long.

"Did you find it yet?" I call out to her.

I find her sitting on her bed, cradling a broken picture frame in her hands. The glass is webbed across the photograph. She slides her fingertips across it, hissing when the sharp edge cuts her.

"Be careful." I grab her wrist, bringing her hand up to my mouth. I lick off the beads of blood and gently suck her finger.

"It's just a little cut," she says softly when I release her finger but continue to stare at her hands.

The nail on her middle finger is broken down below the skin line, and there are scrapes all on the side of her hand. All that clawing in the tower room has damaged her hands.

"You're dangerous to yourself." I drop her hand with a sigh

and take the frame from her. Another photo of her family when she was younger.

"The photo is scratched," she says, getting up from the bed. "I think the note is over here."

She moves to the dresser where there is a stack of books and journals. Pushing them aside, she looks beneath them, then opens the top book.

She retrieves the folded-up paper and brings it to me.

There's a phone number with a cryptic message about the debt being paid upon delivery.

"What does that mean?" I ask. "What debt?"

"The usual kind." She picks up a drawer from the floor and wiggles it back into the dresser while I read the note again.

The number goes nowhere when I try it on my cell.

"Yeah, it wasn't working after I contacted them the first time."

"Explain what that note means. What debt?"

"Credit cards, loans, you know, the usual. They would have paid all of it for me."

"Why would you do that?"

She looks around the room and laughs. "I don't know, maybe someone who doesn't live in a five-thousand-square-foot mansion might want to improve where they live?"

"You want me to believe you put yourself in danger so you could get a nicer apartment?" No way.

She's impulsive, I can sense that, but not for that reason. A new job, more pay, that would get her into a nicer place.

Sneaking into Obsidian for serious money was for a different reason.

"You have what you wanted, now go. I have to clean up this mess." She tries ushering me out of the room, while my phone vibrates several times as text messages come through.

"You're not at all concerned about who did this?" I ask, grabbing my phone.

"I'm more concerned about getting you the hell out of my life." She kicks clothing into a pile in front of her closet door.

I swipe my screen to life and read Ivan's text messages.

"Well, that's not going to happen anytime soon." I look up from my phone.

"What? Why not?" She puts her hands on her hips, staring at me with exasperation.

"Because Dexter Thompson is dead."

Nine

Megan

"He's dead?" My stomach twists. It can't be a coincidence, can it?

"He is." Alexander types on his phone. "Get some things together, we need to go."

I lean against my closet door, taking in a slow breath.

"How did he... how did he die?" My question comes out shaky.

If something horrible happened to him, maybe something horrible is going to happen to me? Maybe something horrible has happened to Mira.

That would explain the radio silence.

My stomach rolls. Sending her away was to keep her safe. Everything is going off the rails.

"I don't know. He collapsed at an event he was at this evening. I will find out more later." He pans the room. "Do you have a suitcase?"

"For what?" Traveling isn't exactly in the budget these days. "You have enough to deal with. I'll just stay here."

"Let me make this clear, Megan, so we can stop the cat and

mouse game you think is happening." He steps over a pile of dirty clothes and comes nose to nose with me. "You have been caught. I'm not chasing."

"I'm not... no." I shake my head with a little laugh. "I can't go with you. I have a life. A real life. A job, friends... uh, a boyfriend!" I blurt that last part out.

The right side of his mouth kicks up to the side. I've amused him.

"You're lying. Again." He runs the back of his knuckles across my jawline up to my ear. "You get flushed right here when you lie, do you know that?"

I'm new to it, so no, I didn't know that. And how can I keep my body from betraying me like mine did earlier?

"If you were telling the truth, if you had a boyfriend, and he let you put yourself in danger the way you have this weekend, I wouldn't let you keep him."

"Let me keep him? You think you have some power there?" Why does this man have the ability to make my heart skip all over my chest and stomp on my last nerve at the exact same time? How am I supposed to be able to think clearly when that's happening?

"I have all the power here," he says.

There's so much force behind his words, in the way he stares at me while he says it, that I completely miss him leaning into me.

His mouth crashes over mine. My body stiffens but melts a microsecond later as his hand wraps around the back of my neck. His lips are warm against mine, sending heated arousal through the rest of my body.

I put my hands against his chest to shove him away, but the tip of his tongue touches my mouth. All protest is gone as I open to him. He deepens the kiss, pressing me against the closet door. The hard length of his cock presses against my hip.

When he breaks away, my lips have to be swollen. There might even be a bruise. I'm too lost to his dark eyes to think about much else other than wanting his touch back.

"I'm in control here, Megan. Everything that happens to you from here on out is up to me."

"What?" I blink a few times, forcing my brain back into action. "What does that mean? And who the hell said that was okay?"

"Until I have all the information I need to be sure you're not a threat, you will be under my care."

"I hear what you're saying, but you make no sense. No one decides for me. No one." I shove him, but it's like trying to move granite. He goes nowhere.

"No one is coming to save you, Megan Reed. And if there was someone who allowed you to put yourself in this situation, I would break their fucking neck for it." He takes a step back, squashing a pair of my jeans beneath his heel.

Great, now I have two mafia bosses wanting to ruin my life.

"Now pack a bag or don't pack a bag. Either way, we're leaving here in five minutes." He snags his phone again, putting it to his ear. "This is Alexander."

Pressed against the door, dazed and angry, I can only watch as he steps over more mess from the break-in and leaves the room.

I could disappear and no one would do anything about it. There would be no big search party. When I don't show up to work, they might try to call me, maybe put in a police report. But the reach of the Volkov family would easily make that go away.

"Who are you?" a male voice demands from the other room.

Billy!

I jump over the piles in my bedroom and hurry down the hall to find the boy who lives on the third floor glaring at Alexander from the doorway. Alexander has one eyebrow arched and looks at me.

"Billy. It's okay. I'm here." I get between them. Billy's barely twenty and lives with his ailing grandmother. He's no threat to anyone.

"Yeah. I just came up to see if... wow, they really made a mess, didn't they?" He surveys the living room.

"They? You saw who did this?" I urge.

"Yeah. They were looking for you, the same guys, you know?" He eyes Alexander, who has now gotten off his phone and moves to stand behind me.

"What guys?" Alexander questions.

Billy looks to me. "You know, *those* guys."

Oh, shit.

"Yeah, I do. Did you talk to them at all?"

"They asked about you. I said I didn't know where you were. They said they were just going to leave a note for you on your door. Guess, they did more than that, huh?" He frowns.

"Who are these men?" Alexander questions again.

"They didn't say anything else?" I press. I'm supposed to have more time. Why would they be here harassing me already?

"Just that they were leaving a note." He blows out a breath.

Alexander puts his hands on my shoulders and gives a little squeeze.

"Still waiting on my answer," he says.

Billy raises his gaze up to Alexander.

"Hey, man. Sorry. I'm Billy. I live up on three with my grandma." He puts his hand out to Alexander, who stares at it.

I try to nudge him.

"Rude asshole," I mutter under my breath, but not soft enough. He must have heard me because he lets me go and takes Billy's hand.

"Alexander Volkov." He pumps Billy's hand, then drops it. "If you know who did this, I'd really like to know." He evens his tone now that he's assessed that Billy isn't a problem.

Billy won't be dragging me away on some white horse to save me from him.

"Volkov? Like the owner of Pulse?" Billy's eyes widen.

Pulse is one of the clubs in my part of town that the Volkov family runs. It's the least upscale of their businesses. A lot of the younger crowd hangs there because the booze is cheap, the bouncers ignore fake IDs, and street drugs flow like a chocolate fountain.

"Yes. That one." Alexander puts on his charm, along with one of his business smiles, and straightens up. "I'm helping Megan with something, and when we stopped home tonight, we found the place like this. So, if you'd tell me who did it, I'd appreciate it."

I try to catch Billy's eye, but he's a little enamored with the successful, charming Alexander Volkov and seems to have completely forgotten me altogether.

"Yeah, man, sure. I'd hoped they'd leave Megan and Mira alone by now, but when I was taking Grandma's laundry downstairs, I ran into the same two guys that come by every month." Billy shakes his head like it's a big shame I've gotten myself into this mess.

Even though I'm not really the one who put me here. I'm just the one who remains stuck here.

"Billy—" I get cut off when Alexander's hands rest on my

shoulders again, closer to my throat this time. He squeezes hard enough to get the warning across.

"Same two men, huh? You have names?" Alexander asks all light and fluffy.

"Nah, never got their names. But they work for Marco DeAngelo, and it's the same two every month." He nods along like he's helping Alexander and is proud to be part of some scheme to keep me safe.

"Marco DeAngelo?" His hands tighten even more. "I've heard of him."

"Not a great guy." Billy nods, then turns his gaze back to me. "Hey, I think I still have your vacuum. You want me to bring it down? I think you're going to need it."

"No, don't worry about it. I have a cleaning crew on the way over," Alexander says.

"Oh. Good. Okay." Billy smiles.

"Thanks, Billy," I say, starting to take a step forward, but Alexander's grip won't soften, so I put my foot back down.

"I'll let you get to it. Let me know if you need anything. Good to meet you, Alexander." Billy grins, then backs out of the apartment, still looking starstruck.

Billy shuts the door.

"Marco DeAngelo?" Alexander spins me around to face him.

I wish he hadn't.

If possible, I swear flames burst in his eyes as he glares down at me.

"Alexander." I lose my nerve to say anything after his name when he puts his hand up.

"Don't." He closes his eyes. "How much?"

"What?"

"How much do you owe the DeAngelo family?" The words are tight and clipped.

"Seventy-five thousand." It might as well be a million with the interest rate they're charging.

"How late are you on the last payment?"

"I only had half the money last month. Technically, I'm a month late on that half, but the regular payment isn't due for another few days." Mira didn't send the money last month like she'd been doing for the past six months.

I slide back a step, but I don't think I can get far enough away to escape his anger.

"Get your things." He has his phone out again and is glaring at the screen. "One minute, Megan. You can go fucking naked for all I care, but we are leaving in one fucking minute."

I hurry out of the living room, his words following me as I turn into my bedroom.

"Yeah. We have a problem."

TEN

ALEXANDER

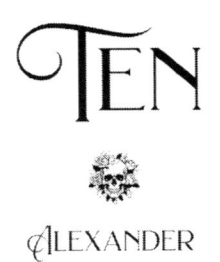

Marco DeAngelo.

Fucking Marco DeAngelo!

"I don't know why you're so pissed at me; I didn't ask you to get involved. I don't *want* you involved. I want you to leave me alone." Megan's words burn my ears as I pull through the gates of my estate.

I should have locked her in the trunk again.

The drive from the city would have been more peaceful.

"Leaving you alone isn't an option." It wasn't much of one to begin with, thanks to her stunt, but now that I know the fucking Italian mob is after her, I really can't let her walk away.

"This has gotten completely out of hand," she mutters and turns away, looking out her window as I pull up to the house.

Once I throw it in park, I shove open my door and jump out. I make it most of the way to her door before she has it open and climbs out.

"My bag." She starts to walk to the trunk, but I grab her arm and tug her toward the steps leading up to the main doors.

"They'll get it. You need to get upstairs. I have people waiting for me." Once we're in the foyer, Yogi greets us.

"Her bag is in the car, so be sure to get it after you park it for the night," I tell him as I drag her toward the large winding staircase. "She's going to be in the yellow suite. Bring it up to her," I instruct, then tug her up the stairs.

"Wait, where is that?" She pulls on my grip. "Not that round room, is it? I won't go back in there, Alexander."

She slaps at me, but I don't answer her.

She can have a fit. Hell, she can throw a whole fucking temper tantrum. I'm not going to respond.

Not because she doesn't deserve the response I'd give, but because if I do it now, while I'm still seeing red, she will bear the marks of my anger. And I won't harm her.

As much as I enjoy hurting her, I will never harm her. It makes no fucking sense, but something about this woman triggers my protective instincts. Not just to keep her safe from the DeAngelo bastards, but herself as well.

In the short chaotic time I've known her, she's managed to grip on to me tight and I'm not sure how easy it will be for me to let go.

If I can let her go.

"Alexander, answer me." She softens her voice as I'm dragging her down the long hallway to the bedroom beside my own.

I push the door open to the room and propel her inside. She catches herself before she falls, then glares at me.

"Answer me," she demands, her eyes narrowed in anger, her fists tight at her sides as her foot stomps quietly against the carpeting.

"You are going to stay in here, Megan. If you step one toe out of this room before I come for you, I will strip you bare and tie you to my bed."

She jerks back.

"Why would you do that?"

"Because you keep forgetting a simple fact." I move toward her with slow deliberate steps. With every inch closer I get, she retreats until the back of her legs hit the massive canopy bed.

I grab hold of her face, pinching her cheeks until they press against her teeth. She winces at what I'm sure is discomfort.

"You are mine now, Megan. Do as I say, and you'll be fine. Step out of line, and you'll learn not to do it again." I push her back a step when I release her and head to the door.

"You have no reason to hate me so much," she says as I grab the door handle to shut the door behind me.

"Are you going to tell me why you borrowed so much fucking money from the DeAngelo family?"

I wait, watching the wheels turn in that beautiful fucking head of hers. There's already a pink blotch growing on her throat, telling me nothing she says will be true.

At the last moment, she decides to evade the question instead. "It's none of your business."

I squelch the desire to throw her across the bed and force her to tell me everything. The anger is too raw right now.

"Everything about you is my business now, Megan. When I get back, you are going to tell me every last fucking detail of the trouble you're actually in."

Her eyes narrow on me. "I don't want to be here. I don't want to be with you."

"You gave up all hope of ever getting what you want when you trespassed and tried to take what didn't belong to you."

She screws her face into a glower.

"Not one toe." I remind her and yank the door shut,

leaving her alone in the bedroom and me outside in the hall, willing my anger at her recklessness to calm.

Something hits the other side of the door.

I almost smile, but then I remember the name Marco DeAngelo and grit my teeth as I make my way down to my office.

※

"WHAT THE HELL HAPPENED?" I ask the moment I step into my office where Ivan and Kaz are helping themselves to my brandy.

Kaz sits in an armchair, one arm draped over the rolled leather arm and one foot hooked over his opposite knee.

"He's dead." The crystal decanter top clinks as Ivan drops it in place.

"Yes. I understood your text. How?" I join him at the bar tucked into the corner of the office and pour three fingers of brandy for myself.

"He collapsed." Kaz gestures with his hand. "One minute he was standing there, telling a boring story, the next he was flat on his back, eyes rolled to the back of his head." He mimics the motion with his arm, making it look like a tree fell in the woods.

"Why did he collapse?" I down half my drink, trying to wash away the irritation the distracting woman upstairs has caused.

"Don't know yet. The coroner said we'd have a cause of death by morning." Ivan brings his glass to the couch. "Nothing happened. The man just keeled over and died."

"Dexter Thompson was thirty-five years old, Ivan. How does a thirty-five-year-old just drop dead?" I question. Two years younger than me, and he's just gone in a breath. It's unnerving.

"He did have some heart condition," Kaz offers. "Last year, when we were in that meeting with him for the build on the west side, he stopped in the middle of talking about a contribution to some organization to get a pill bottle out of his drawer. He said it was for his heart."

"Okay, so say his heart gave out. There's nothing to worry about, then. Right?" Ivan questions.

If only that were the case. But there's a woman upstairs whose involvement with Marco DeAngelo suggests Thompson's death is more than just natural causes. The timing is too coincidental. And I don't believe in coincidences.

"We'll have to wait until we get the cause of death. Even if he did die of natural causes, we still have someone who was trying to get information on him." I grab the folded-up paper out of my pocket, unfold the thick stationery, and hand it to Ivan.

He sits up straighter, noticing right away the emblem watermarked on the back. It's subtle. Someone who wasn't looking for it would probably miss it.

The Obsidian logo.

Ivan's eyebrows shoot up, then he hands it to Kaz, who frowns.

"Debts will be repaid?" Kaz reads the top of the stationery. "What is this?"

"That's what Megan Reed was given as an introduction to the job of sneaking into our records room." I finish off my drink and pour another, dropping a ball of ice from the bucket.

"I assume you called this number." Kaz waves the paper.

"I did. No longer in service." I lean against my desk.

"It worked when she called it, though?" Ivan questions with

a wrinkled forehead. "And where was she supposed to drop it off?"

"They were supposed to send drop-off instructions, but she didn't get them." I take a breath. "When I took her back to her place tonight to get the note, her apartment had been turned over," I explain.

"Turned over? You think the person behind this did it?" Kaz asks.

"No." I put my drink down and grip the edge of my desk as I lean back against it. "I think Marco DeAngelo's men did it."

"Marco DeAngelo?" Ivan's jaw tightens. "That Italian fuck who sells that laced shit on the streets?"

"Yeah, that's the one. That's his main money, but in this case, it's his loan business that's got her in a mess," I explain.

"He lent her money?" Kaz questions. "How much?"

"She owes seventy-five grand."

"What did she need with that kind of money?" Ivan questions.

"Not sure yet." I will have my answers by morning, though. "But she says credit card debt."

I grab my drink, wishing it could give me some relief from the stress of the day. But the little burn from the brandy is nothing compared to the irritation and lust I'm fighting, thanks to that black-haired pixie with the most unusual white streaks sulking upstairs.

I should tie her to my bed and take my belt to her ass again for being such a damn distraction.

Just thinking of it only makes my cock hard again.

"So she hasn't given you much in the way of answers?" Ivan grins, the bastard.

"You think this is funny."

He nods.

"I think it's amusing, yes. Alexander Volkov hasn't been able to squash a simple problem like this within twenty-four hours?" He chuckles. "Where is she now?"

"Where do you think?" I ask with a heavy sigh.

"In your bed?" Kaz winks.

"No." I clench my teeth. "She's upstairs. I came down to get you two up to speed and find out what happened with Dexter. Now that I have, I'll deal with her and get this whole fucking thing resolved."

"Hmmm." Kaz gets to his feet. "I'm sure it will be that easy."

I shove off the desk. "You two can see yourselves out."

I grit my teeth. They're right. I should have had this wrapped up. I've let her get away too long without giving me all the answers she has wrapped up in her little mind.

If she had been a man, she wouldn't be tucked into a warm bed tonight. She'd be hanging from the ceiling in the pit.

I've been too soft.

I climb the stairs, flexing and clenching my hands.

That ends.

She's going to tell me exactly why she borrowed that money from the DeAngelo family. And she's going to retrace every fucking step she took since she found that letter on her desk.

The lights in the hallway are dimmed, but I see the bedroom door clearly, and my resolve is set as stone.

No more half answers.

She will tell me everything and I will fix this fucking problem and get back to my fucking life.

I get to the door of the room I left her in and throw it open, expecting to find her lying in the bed or pacing the room.

My blood runs cold at the sight before me.

The window is open, the fall night breeze blowing the curtains into the room.

There is no sign of Megan Reed.

She's gone.

ELEVEN

MEGAN

Leaves crunch beneath my feet as I hurry through the wooded landscaping of Alexander's house. Fire erupts in my ankle with each step, but I force myself to keep moving.

Climbing down the side of his house wasn't as hard as I'd thought it would be, but the last jump to the garden patio twisted my ankle. I'm sure it's swelling, but I don't have time to stop and look.

It's cloudy tonight, so I have to rely on any lighting I can see from the street to lead the way. Except I can't see the street yet.

The driveway was long, but not so long I shouldn't be able to get to the street before Alexander comes looking for me. If I keep moving, the streetlamps should come into view soon.

"Megan!" Alexander's roar shakes the ground.

No! I need more time.

I freeze, sure he's spotted me, but when I glance over my shoulder, I don't see him.

I quicken my pace, my gaze darting around for the best path out.

Gotta move faster, get farther away from the house.

Pain slices up my leg—this fucking limp isn't helping.

Move, Megan, move!

I can't be here. I can't wait for him to decide what to do with me.

It's bad enough having one mob boss on my ass about the money he says I owe him. I can't have another mafia family putting me on their shit list.

"Megan!" Fuck. I limp faster, dragging my right foot more than using it.

I can't see the fence line or any streetlamps. I must still be too far away from the main road. Where the hell does he live? We aren't far enough away from the city to have this much landscape.

A gunshot rings out and I fall to the ground, pressing my cheek to the leaves and dirt. The lunatic is shooting at me!

"You have fifteen seconds to surrender yourself." His voice carries his demand easily through the trees.

There is no way that's happening. I remember his threat, and the darkness that swam in his eyes when he gave it. I'll take my chances out here. The only thing for me to do is get out of this place.

I can't go home, but that's fine. Maybe I can stay with Bella for a few days. I haven't spoken to her since she moved out of the city, but I'm sure she'll let me crash on her couch.

Billy and his grandmother are another option, but Billy would cave in a heartbeat if Alexander came around with questions.

Another shot.

Fuck!

"Ten seconds!" he bellows. He's no closer than before, I think.

He's not coming after me; he's fully expecting me to come to him.

Well, he can hold his breath waiting for that to happen. Pushing myself to get moving, I hurry as best I can, ignoring the white-hot pain shooting up my leg every time I step on my right foot.

Something stubs my toe, and I fly forward face-first into the dead leaves and dirt on the ground. A root tripped me. At least I didn't twist my good ankle.

"Five seconds!" His bellow blows through the trees. More leaves fall in the darkness and land on my head.

Looking around, I try to find a place to hide. There's nothing but trees as far as I can see. Maybe I've gone the wrong way.

A fallen tree trunk isn't far away, so I crawl to it as twigs bite my knees. Not changing out of this damn dress before embarking on my escape is yet another bad decision among a mountain of other bad decisions I've made recently.

Climbing over the thick trunk, I flatten myself against the ground. I take long, deep breaths trying to get my heart to slow. It's beating so hard; I'm sure Alexander will hear it in the silence of the night.

Counting in my head, I hit the number five, then ten, then thirty. Where is he?

Focusing all my energy on listening, I try to place him, but there's not a sound. No leaves crunching, no twigs breaking, nothing.

Could he have given up and gone back inside?

Silently, I count the seconds. But the sound of my own panic bubbling in my ears makes me lose my number and I have to start over again. Only when I'm confident several minutes have passed without any sound from him do I chance taking a peek.

The bark of the fallen tree is rough against my palms as I use it to push up just enough to see over it.

Nothing.

He probably realized I'm more trouble than I'm worth, a note I've been given more than a few times in my life, and went back inside. More than likely, he'll assume I'm going home and he'll just catch up to me at my apartment.

Sighing with relief, I sink back down behind the trunk and roll over to my back.

A set of dark eyes shimmer with the little light from the moon peeking through the tree branches. Before I can scream, he slaps a hand over my mouth, crouching in front of me.

"Naughty, naughty girl." He scoots closer. "I told you to come back, but you wanted to run." His breath is hot against my cheek.

Beneath his hand I try to shake my head.

"No?" he huffs. "But you did run, Megan. You wanted me to chase you, so I did. And now you've been caught."

Pushing against the ground, I try to shove away from him, but my hand slips with the leaves and I nearly hit my head on the trunk of the tree. He catches me, cradling my head in his hand.

"Hmm, there are so many ways I'm going to punish you." Coming even closer, he inhales, probably sensing my fear. A man like him probably gets off on other people's terror.

His lips spread wide in an arrogant grin.

"I'm going to pull my hand away, and all you're allowed to say is 'Yes, sir' or 'No, sir.'" He pauses, waiting for me to respond, I guess, so I nod beneath his hand.

Gingerly, he peels his hand away and I lick my lips, tasting him. Again, I try to scramble back from him, but the tree behind me is blocking me. There's nowhere else to go, and he's still glaring at me.

"Now that I've caught you, what to do with you?" He tilts his head a little. It's not a question; he's just trying to freak me out.

It's working.

Trailing his finger down the side of my cheek, he pushes away my hair, tucking it behind my ear.

"You have a cut on your cheek." He sounds angry about it.

Just wait until he sees my ankle, and what a mess my knees probably are from the twigs and my fall.

"Yes, sir," I say quietly when the time ticks by, and he still hasn't said anything else.

He glances down the length of my torso. There's a tear in the dress where I got caught up in the bushes after landing on the patio. He pokes at it, slipping his finger through it and skimming his fingertip along my stomach.

"You shouldn't have ran."

"I'll never stop trying to get away from you." I push his hand away from me, tearing the dress a little more as his finger gets caught in the hole. "I won't just let you keep me here."

His eyes narrow in on me.

"I will catch you. And every time I do, the punishment will be worse." He moves closer, moving one knee between my legs.

"Just let me go," I whisper as he leans in, his forehead touching mine.

"I can't." He inhales. "I won't."

His mouth crashes over mine, claiming me in a possessive kiss that leaves no question as to his intentions. Panic rises in my chest, and I try to shove him away. Maybe I can still get free of this place.

Of him.

But it's like trying to move Mt. Everest. In response, he deepens the kiss, wrapping his hand around the back of my neck and squeezing firmly.

I'm not going anywhere without his permission; he's getting that point across loud and clear.

He leaves me breathless, swimming in a pool of arousal and all he did was kiss me. It's obviously been way too long since I've had a man in my bed if just a kiss, no matter how deep, possessive, and downright sexy can make me a gooey mess.

His fingers play with the drawstring of the dress. Too easily, he tugs on the string, and it unties, opening the neckline enough for the top of my breasts to be exposed. I try to grab it, to keep it shut, but he raises his eyebrow while brushing away my hand, and it's as if I have no power over my own damn body.

"Someone will see." Reason. Surely, he'll see reason. We're outside!

"If you were worried about that, you should have stayed in the house." His voice darkens. "Where I told you to stay." He lowers his mouth, kissing my neck, nipping at my earlobe.

With his other hand, he trails up my leg, stopping at my knee.

A low growl echoes in my ear.

"You've scratched your legs to hell," he accuses, moving his touch farther up to my thighs. "You're hot and wet," he grumbles as he palms my sex.

Before I can defend myself, as if there is a defense for how easily my body reacts to him, he grabs hold of the elastic of my panties and yanks. The material tears easily and simply falls away to the forest floor.

"Alexander." I try to scoot away, but he's too strong, too big, and he's back to kissing me. His hands sink into my hair, and I'm lost to his strength.

"You shouldn't have run." He breaks away, grabbing my arms and hoisting me from the pile of leaves I'm lying in and flips me face down over the fallen tree.

Dammit.

"What? No!" I hear the belt buckle jingling. "Please! No!"

"You could have killed yourself jumping from that height." He grabs my hips, easily tossing the skirt of the dress up over my ass. My bare ass.

I try to scramble, but my left foot slips in the leaves, and my right foot hurts too much to be of any use now that I've been off it for a few minutes.

The leather strap drops in front of my eyes and wraps around my neck. He slides the other end through the buckle and pulls tight, creating a collar with leash around my throat. I pull at the leather, but he's tugging it tight from behind me.

Palming my bare ass, he squeezes.

"You're going to learn. If you need to learn the hard way, that's on you." In the next second, his hand connects, and I'm pushed forward on the log. He brings it down a second time and then stills.

Sensing a moment of hesitation, I try to lurch over the log, but he still has my neck in his belt, and I can't get anywhere.

He runs his hand over my ass cheek, then lower, and lower still, until his fingers slide easily through my slick sex.

I groan.

Not only because it feels so damn good to have him touch me, but because he can see how good it feels.

The arrogant man doesn't need more coaxing to strengthen his ego.

One thick finger penetrates me, then a second.

"Alexander. Please." I press my palms into the dirt and leaves to keep from rolling off the log and falling face-first onto the ground.

"Please, what? Please make you feel good? Or please punish you for being such a naughty girl?" His question gets lost in the pleasure of his fingers stroking me, slowly pumping in and out of my pussy.

He curls his fingers inside me, and it's too much to ignore.

"Please... this is wrong."

He leans over me, the warmth and strength of his body pressing me into the rough bark of the log. "Everything about me is wrong."

Not exactly comforting words.

"But this." He sweeps his free hand around my waist, easily finding my sensitive, swollen clit. "This will never be wrong."

I clench my teeth, but it does nothing to hold back the pleasure-filled moan that erupts when he pinches my clit.

The belt goes slack around my throat, but the weight of it is enough to remind me of its presence.

"Fuck, your pussy is so tight, so hot, so wet." His fingers are gone in the next second and I whine.

Whine!

His clothing shifts and the thick head of his cock presses against my entrance.

I freeze.

"Reach behind and spread your ass cheeks wide," he directs me, and I'm sure the entire forest will start on fire from the flames in my cheeks.

I can't do what he says. I can't.

"The longer you take to obey, the longer I keep your release from you," he promises.

"I... please don't make me." I shake my head, but he probably can't see me with the darkness as I dangle over the other side of the log.

"I'm not making you. It's a choice. Obey or not. The consequences of that are up to you." He pushes the tip of his cock against my pussy, just barely breaking through the entrance.

The belt tightens around my throat again, reminding me I'm not going anywhere. There is no getting away from Alexander until he lets me go.

Mentally kicking myself, I reach back and do as he orders. I pull my ass cheeks apart.

"Good girl," he coos, and my pussy gets even wetter.

Betrayal. Every bit of my body betrays me.

"Hold this position until I say otherwise," he instructs, while dropping the end of the makeshift leash and grabbing my hips.

I can barely register his words before he plows into me. The stretch is too much, and I cry out.

"Careful," he grounds out as though his teeth are clenched. "Hold still. It will ease up in a second."

I drop my head. I'm full, so damn full. His fingers work over my clit again, rubbing in a soft circle, morphing the discomfort into desire.

"Ah, there you are." He continues petting my clit while dragging his cock back, almost all the way out of my pussy. I nearly lose my grip on my cheeks when he plows back in.

"So good." He pinches my clit, then quickly switches to a soft touch, rubbing two fingers in methodically slow circles, driving me to the edge as his cock thrusts into me again and again.

Darkness fogs the edge of my vision as his fingers continue to dance the most erotic dance and he thrusts upward, hitting a new spot I've never felt before.

I jolt and cry out.

Fuck, I've never felt that. It was so, so, so... he does it again and I scream.

"That's a good girl," he says again. "Don't let go of your cheeks. Just feel... fuck, you're so tight, so hot... fuck." He thrusts harder and harder, and I do my best to lift up to meet him each time.

I barely notice the log beneath me or the humiliation of holding my ass cheeks spread open for him anymore. It's only pleasure.

Unmeasurable amounts of pleasure warm my skin, my blood. Every part of me is lost to the sensations he's drowning me in.

I should be fighting him off. I wanted to, but his fingers, his kiss, his touch, it's like the moment he touches me, my body becomes his to command, and I lose all power over it.

"Should I let you come? After you've been such a bad girl? Should I?" He thrusts harder.

I don't want to answer. I can't give in. Even if I've already given over completely, I have to keep this part to myself.

But he won't be denied.

"Or should I keep you dangling on the edge?" His hands on my hips tighten, the tips of his fingers digging into my flesh. It only makes everything better, the bite of pain he gives me. "I'll bring you right to the point of release and deny you over and over and over."

The threat itself brings me closer to oblivion. My core tightens. I'm a pistol ready to fire.

"I can keep that up for hours. Your pussy will be so sore, so empty, you'll beg me to stop, to give you what you want." He puts more pressure on my clit. "But I won't. So, choose. Obey me in this or don't."

Everything clenches. I'm so close to losing my mind, I can barely get the words out that he wants to hear.

"Yes. Please! Please let me come." I throw my head back with a cry as his fingers push me right to the edge. "I'm sorry. I'm sorry, please let me."

"Sorry for what?" He's toying with me, using my own body against me. Knowing that I'd probably say anything right now to get what he is withholding.

"I'm sorry for trying to run."

"For being a..." His words trail off, leaving me to finish the sentence.

"I'm sorry for being a bad girl." My face heats. Hell, my entire body warms as the words fly from my mouth. But I don't care. I just need him, more of him, all of him. I need him to pull the trigger and let me explode.

He leans over me, filling me further, in a new angle that hits perfectly.

"Good girl. Come for me, Megan. Show me what a good girl you are." His fingernails dig into my hips.

I lift up, arching my back and giving him more of my body as he pummels into me. And as though my body were waiting for his command, I come completely unglued beneath his touch.

My throat stretches around my scream as my orgasm tears through me.

"Such a good girl!" He plows harder, faster, twisting his hips and driving into me, driving me straight through my orgasm.

The intensity knocks the breath from my lungs.

I've never been so completely depleted before. My hands fall away to my sides.

"Fuck. Fuck," he groans, twisting his hips and thrusting harder and harder.

I'm pushed farther over the log, and I stop myself from falling with my hands. Twigs bite into my palms.

Another thrust and another, and then he stills, letting a roar of pleasure loose into the woods.

Animals will be too scared to come out for days after the amount of noise we've made here tonight.

"Megan." His raw voice breaks through the silence.

"Yeah?" I push up from the log as he leans back, sliding his cock out of me and letting his hot cum slip out of me and down my thigh.

"You let go."

TWELVE

ALEXANDER

This woman makes me forget who I am. It only takes a simple look from her, and I turn into a lustful, undisciplined teenager. More eager to get my cock inside her than to teach her a lesson she so rightly deserves.

I pocket her panties that are in tatters on the ground, then help her to roll off the log. Dead leaves and dirt cling to my slacks at the knees. Only this woman could make me ruin a perfectly good pair of pants to fuck in the mud.

"I got it." She lightly pushes my hands away when I try to help her get to her feet.

I get out of her way while I zip up. My belt still hangs around her neck. The dark, worn leather nestled against the creamy, soft skin of her throat looks almost natural. Like her wearing my mark in any way is exactly as things should be.

As though hearing my thoughts, she reaches for it.

"No." I grab her wrist and put it at her side. "It stays."

Anger flashes in her eyes.

"This wasn't enough of a punishment?" She throws her hand around, gesturing to the log.

"No," I say simply, not explaining that an orgasm isn't a punishment—no matter if I tried to make it sound like it was. My ego needed appeasing, and justifying fucking the woman instead of tying her up in the pit was necessary.

For me.

If I can't explain it to her, at least I can be honest with myself.

Even when the truth darkens my mood further.

"Let's go." I grab her elbow and start walking. It only takes a few steps to realize she's hurt.

As I turn to see what the problem is, she merely bats her eyes at me. Her stubbornness is going to make me lose my mind.

I grab my phone from my back pocket and hit the flashlight feature. As soon as the beam sweeps across her right foot, my blood instantly boils.

It's swollen up to the size of a softball. At least there's no bruising, but she's barely putting any weight on it.

"It's fine." Again, she tries to swat my hands away when I reach for her, but it doesn't work this time.

"Hold on to me." I sweep her up into my arms and wait for her to put her arms around my neck.

"I can walk," she argues.

"No, you can't." Leaves crunch beneath my steps as I take her out of the woods and back to the house.

"We're still in the backyard?" She lifts her head when the back patio that she landed on comes into view.

"The back of my property backs up to the woods. You weren't even on my property anymore when I found you." If she'd kept going in the direction she was headed, it would have taken her another hour, maybe longer with her ankle, to get to a main road.

"Oh. I thought I made my way to the front of the house," she huffs. "My sense of direction must be off."

"I'm beginning to think you have no sense at all," I mutter.

Gregor opens the back patio door for me, letting us into the house.

"Get the doctor here," I order and take her to the stairs. "I'll be in my room."

She stiffens in my arms.

"No, my room. Put me in my room. And I don't need a doctor."

I tighten my hold on her.

"Don't argue, Megan. Not now. Not when you've made me angry again."

"How'd I do that?" she questions as I start up the stairs. "I did what you said. I... you know."

I let myself take a glance at her.

The blush on her cheeks makes me want to take her all over again.

"You didn't tell me you were hurt." I kick the door to my room open and head to the adjoining bathroom.

"Would you have not done what you did?"

I gently put her on the bathroom counter. Now in the well-lit room, I see the damage this woman did to herself.

Aside from the scratch on her cheek and the ankle she may have broken, her legs are scratched to hell. And she's filthy.

I ignore her question, not sure I have the answer she wants to hear. Would it have stopped me from turning her over that log and taking what I've wanted to take since I saw her standing in the office at Obsidian?

I don't know.

"Stay here." I point my finger at her and wait for a small nod from her before I step away and gather a few washcloths and supplies to clean her cuts.

"I can do this." She reaches for the washcloth as I turn on the water in the sink.

"No." Once the water is warm enough, I soak the washcloth and grab the antibacterial soap.

"It's just a few scrapes," she says, bending over to look at her legs, stretching them out so she can get a better look.

"Hmm." Standing in front of her, I take hold of her left foot and press it against my hip. Her knees took most of the damage. Carefully, I brush away all the little bits of twigs and dead leaves that cling to her skin.

Most of the scratches are superficial, but there's one gash with debris lodged in it. Reaching over to the counter where I put my supplies, I grab the pair of tweezers.

She stiffens.

"Maybe you should let the doctor do this?" She goes to move her leg away, but I merely place my hand over her knee.

"He's not touching you other than to look at your ankle." This wound is just above her knee, dangerously close to her thigh. Unless this thing needs stitches, he's not touching her here.

"Why?" She bumps into my head as she bends over again to watch me pluck out the tiny pieces of branch.

I look up at her. "Because." Gently, I nudge her head away. "You're blocking my light."

"Oh." She leans back.

The silence stretches while I finish cleaning out the debris.

"Did you find out what happened to that guy?" she asks after I drop the tweezers back onto the countertop and reach for the peroxide.

"Dexter? He's dead." The peroxide bubbles over the cut. She hisses, grabbing on to my shoulder and squeezing.

"Shit! That hurts!" She tries to pull her leg away, but I hold firm. "Are you sure you know what you're doing?"

"My grandmother used to clean my cuts like this when I was a little boy. It stings, but it works." Grabbing one of the bandages, I carefully place it over the cut.

"I can't imagine you being a little boy," she says.

She's staring at me with narrowed eyes. Like she's trying to conjure up the image of me as a young kid running down the street, playing with a bunch of schoolkids.

"I may not have had a typical childhood, but I assure you, I was a kid once."

"It was a long time ago, though. I'm sure medicines have changed since then." She waves her hand over the wound, like the cool, moving air is going to make it better.

"Is that a jab at my age?" I squeeze her calf.

"Well, you are almost forty." She looks up at me with a sarcastic grin.

"Not quite there yet." I run my thumbs over the edges of the bandage to be sure it's firmly in place.

"How did he die?" she asks.

"What?"

"The guy. How did he die?" The topics change like the breeze with her.

"He collapsed. We'll know more tomorrow." I gently put her foot down and carefully pick up her other leg, careful not to touch her ankle. These cuts are all superficial, so it's easier to clean them up without causing her any more pain.

"So, natural causes. I can go home, then." She sounds so damn hopeful; it's almost a shame I have to shatter it.

Almost.

"No."

"Why not?" She looks ready to hop off the counter, so I put my hands on her hips and keep her firmly in place as I lean closer to her.

"Because."

"That's not an answer."

"It's the one you're getting." I reach around her and start tugging on the dress, trying to pull it up over her hips, but she wiggles.

"What are you doing?"

"The dress is dirty, and I need to see if you have any cuts on your stomach. There's a hole here." I finger the tear in the fabric. "I assume this happened when you jumped into the bushes?"

The mental image of it makes my blood heat again, so I shove it away.

"I'll check myself." She tries to swat my hands away when I reach around her again.

Clenching my teeth, I sigh. Fighting with her is going to waste time, and the doctor will be here soon.

Decision made, I grab the neckline of the dress and tear straight down the middle, shredding the thin material in half.

"What the hell!" She grabs for what's left, trying to pull it back together.

"I don't have time to argue with you over everything. Just sit here for a minute." I give her a look that seems to do the trick, then run my hands over her shoulders as I shove the dress off.

Fuck.

Me.

The woman is a glory.

There's only one scratch on her stomach, a thin one where the branch tore the dress. But I take my time inspecting her stomach, gently running my fingertips over her ribs.

Her nipples pebble when my attention moves to her breasts. Cupping them, I rub my thumbs over her nipples. A small sigh escapes her pretty lips.

93

"Alexander!" Gregor's voice cuts through the room like an axe splintering wood.

"Fuck." I release her and go to the bathroom door, keeping it mostly closed to hide the naked beauty sitting on my bathroom counter.

"Oh. There you are. The doctor's here." He jerks a head behind him where the doctor is probably standing.

"Fine. Let him in. I'll bring her out."

When I get back to her, she's trying to put the dress back on.

"You're not wearing that thing; it's dirty and torn up." I grab it from her and toss it in the trash can.

"Well, who tore it?" she accuses.

"Who decided to be a bad girl and jump into a fucking rosebush?" I work the buttons of my shirt open and pull it from my pants.

"What are you doing?" She swallows as I take the shirt off, leaving me in my white undershirt.

"You need to cover up." I drape the shirt over her shoulders and wait for her to work her arms into the sleeves before I start buttoning it up. She's drowning in the shirt, but I like her wearing it. It's mine and so is she.

She tries again to hop off the counter, so I grab her hips and shove her back down.

"If you keep trying to jump off this counter, the doctor is going to hear you getting your ass smacked. Then you'll have trouble walking and sitting." I level her with a dark glare that should send chills down her spine, but all she does is frown.

"Fine. But at least let me walk on my own."

"No." I don't negotiate. At some point, she'll learn that.

In the meantime, I scoop her off the counter and carry her into the bedroom where Doctor Kowalik waits for us.

The covers of the bed have been pulled down already, so I slip her into bed. With her bad leg out, I cover the rest of her with the blanket, earning a heavy sigh and an eye roll from her.

"Oh, wow. You really did a number here, didn't you?" The doctor pushes his thin-framed glasses up his nose and starts his inspection of her ankle. As soon as he touches the swelling, she jumps.

"I can put some pressure on it, but not much," she tells him.

I stand behind him as he continues to poke and prod at it, gritting my teeth every time she hisses from the pain. It's necessary, I tell myself, but that doesn't make me any less pissed off that he's hurting her.

"Well, I don't think it's broken. I can meet you down at the office if you'd like to do an X-ray to be sure, though." He looks over his shoulder at me.

"It's not broken," she interjects. "It's not even that bad."

"Does she need to stay off it?" I keep my focus on the doctor and not the horrible patient already trying to climb out of bed.

"For at least a day, maybe more depending on her comfort. If the swelling goes down and she can put weight on it, she'll be fine. But if she can't stand on it within a few days, bring her in so we can be certain she hasn't torn any ligaments." The doctor opens the black case he brought and pulls out a bottle, handing it to me. "For the pain. One every six hours if she needs it."

I take it with a nod.

"She needs something now, something that will work faster. You got something like that?"

He looks in his case.

"I do." He nods and leans closer to me, dropping his voice.

"It will sedate her, though. It's a heavy medication. When they called, I assumed it was one of you boys who got hurt. She'll sleep clear through tomorrow morning."

I eye her over his shoulder. Clearly annoyed we're talking about her, she's glaring at me.

My lip curls. "Do it."

Thirteen

Megan

Three days.

The man has left me in this room alone for three days.

He's been nice enough to send staff in with food every few hours, and plenty of it, and it's all been beyond delicious. But that's beside the point.

He let that doctor drug me and then just left me here.

I haven't even seen him, not that I want to see him. He's not bad to look at, but it's hard to demand your release when your captor refuses to come around.

Well, today is the day I'm getting the hell out of here. I've missed work, so who knows if I even have a job now. And Marco is going to come looking for me soon.

I have nothing to offer him. Dread fills me at the thought of our next conversation, but before it consumes me and freezes me up, I have to act right now.

Enough is enough. I've never been one to just sit around and wait for someone to come save me.

No one's coming. Life has been a cruel teacher, stealing

away my father when I was only twelve and then slowly dragging my mother to her grave when the ink on my high school diploma was still wet. But I've learned my lesson well.

I'm on my own, and that means saving myself.

Finding my bag in the closet, I dig out a pair of leggings and a long-sleeved t-shirt and get dressed. I throw open the bedroom door, ready to fight whatever guard is sitting outside.

There's no one.

I'd just assumed Alexander would have someone posted outside the room, and with my ankle being in such bad shape for the past few days, I hadn't exactly been able to make a run for it.

With my bag strapped over my shoulder, I march as confidently as I can down the hall to the wide winding staircase that he'd carried me up days ago. Stopping every few steps to listen for voices, I get down them as quickly as I can.

"What are you doing?" Alexander's voice hits me as soon as I'm in the foyer. The front door is right there. Only a few more steps.

I drag in a deep breath, rolling my shoulders back and throwing my chin up as I turn to face him.

"I'm going home. Enough is enough. I have a job, hopefully, and a life." And an entirely different mob boss to placate in order to keep Mira and myself alive.

I shift my weight to my left foot. Even with the swelling down and the pain only a slight dull ache, I don't want to take any chances on making it worse.

Alexander is dressed in a pair of black slacks with a black button-down shirt tucked into them. His belt hugs his hips, and for a moment I can feel the heaviness of it on my neck again. I have to stop myself from reaching up to touch the skin there.

He hooks his hands on his hips and stares at me, his jaw

getting tighter by the moment. The sleeves of his shirt are rolled up to his elbows, exposing the dark tattoos covering his forearms.

"You're right." He gives a curt nod, making his way to me. "Enough is enough."

I'm barely able to register his movements as he grabs my bag from me and tosses it to the ground.

"This way." He cups my elbow and urges me along with him.

"Alexander." I try to tug away from him, but he tightens his grip. "What are you doing? Let me go."

"I'm going to show you something, Megan." He brings me down one hallway, then another and another. This place is an absolute maze. I'm completely turned around by the time he brings me to a door.

He has to unlock it with a key before opening it, then gestures for me to climb down the stairs ahead of him.

I give a little shake of my head. It's dark down there, and that door had been locked. How do I know he's not going to just lock me away since I'm not giving up on leaving?

His heavy sigh blows through my hair as he leans over me to hit the light switch. The stairwell illuminates and there's a dim glow at the bottom.

"Go." He nudges my back when I still stand frozen.

I don't really have a choice. I know that. He'll just drag me down there if he wants me there.

Slowly, I climb down the wooden steps into a basement. The door shuts behind me with a clank. It sounds more like a jail cell slamming than an ordinary basement door. I pause to look back over my shoulder. He's right there, coming with me.

"To the left," he says when I reach the bottom and can step in two directions.

Another light flickers on as I take cautious steps over the cement floor. Air whooshes from my lungs.

It's just a basement. Boxes stashed on shelves line the outer wall. The musty smell from years of storage fills the room.

"Down here." He guides me with his hand on the small of my back when we reach another hallway.

There's another locked door that we move through. The hallway narrows, like we're in a passageway between buildings or something instead of his basement. It's colder in here. I don't think we're in any part of his house anymore.

A chill runs over my skin when we come to another door. Unlike the other typical wooden doors, this one is made of steel. There are three locks on it, and a deadbolt.

"Wait." I grab on to his wrist when he goes to slide the deadbolt open. "What's... why are we down here?"

He ignores my question and slides the lock open. The metal scraping against the bolt screeches in the dead silence of the passageway. I have to step back when he pulls the door open toward us. It's thick, almost like a vault door.

There's nothing but darkness inside, yet goosebumps cover my arms and the little hairs on the back of my neck stand at attention. Evil happens here, and I don't need a light to show me that.

"Go on in." He flips a light switch on the outside of the room, lighting up the room. It's empty. "Megan. Go. Inside."

"I don't want to," I whisper. Fear keeps my feet planted. If I go in there, I might not come out.

His warm touch to the back of my neck does little to melt the icy terror in control of my thoughts.

"I thought I made it clear already, but let me explain again. I don't care what you want." There's a sharp edge to his tone, like I've pushed him far enough.

With small, hesitant steps, I make my way inside the room.

Just like the tower room he had me in that first night, this room is completely round. The walls are cement and painted a dull gray, the floor the same. Except this room has what that one didn't.

A hook dangles from the ceiling in the center, and below that a drain in the floor.

I jump away from the grate and hurry to a wall, pressing my back to the cold cement.

"I'm sorry," I say.

Alexander prowls around the room, his pace unhurried until he stops in front of me. He plants his arms on either side of me, caging me against the wall.

He left the door open, but it doesn't matter. Even if I manage to slip out before he catches me, the front door is too far. I'd never make it—not with the soreness still lingering in my ankle.

"It's time you answer some questions, Megan."

"I already told you what I know." My voice trembles and I hate it. I hate how easily the darkness in his eyes can make me question my strength.

"Not about Dexter." His brow wrinkles. "I want to know about Marco DeAngelo. Why do you owe him so much money?"

Of course he does. Marco works within an entirely different family. Anything Alexander can use against him would probably come in handy for when they do whatever they do.

"I can handle Marco on my own," I tell him.

His lips curl inward.

"No. You can't." He leans closer. "Megan, do you know what happens in this room?"

"Nothing good," I answer.

The metal hook, like the ones butchers use to hang a side

of beef, dangles just behind him. I may not know the details of Alexander's business, but I can imagine well enough what they do to people in here.

"Not for the people I leave in here, no." His touch is light as he pushes my hair back from my face, tucking it behind my ear. "I'm going to ask you again, why do you owe Marco DeAngelo money?"

I'm locked in his gaze. It's like a weight pulling me down and I'm too tired to struggle against it.

He'll keep me here until I tell him. Maybe he will lock me in here; maybe he'll hang me from that hook and do horrible things to me.

If he finds out about Mira, he could send his henchmen to find her, and it could be her hanging from the hook. He can use her against Marco. Or he could hand her over to Marco in exchange for some territory deal.

I wish I understood his world better, then I could prepare for all possible scenarios and play this game better. All I know is he's not some knight in shining armor. He's all power and dominance. He wears danger in the same manner most men wear aftershave.

"Mira owes the money," I finally say. "My roommate."

"Then why are you making payments to him? Where is she?"

"She's out of town." I take a small breath. "She sends me money, and I pay Marco."

He searches my face, like he's not sure if he should believe me or not.

"There's more. What is it?" he questions, his eyes roaming over my face and neck. "Why are you covering for her?"

All I can do is hope the high collar of my sweater will cover any physical tells. I'm not lying, but I'm not giving him everything. I may not know how to play these games as well as he does, but I know enough to keep a few cards close to my chest.

"Because she's my family," I explain in terms he can understand. "I would do anything to keep her safe, to help her when she needs it. And she'd do the same for me."

He's a big player in the mafia; words like family and loyalty mean something to him. Even if words like legal and morality don't.

His jaw tightens. "You put yourself in the middle of a mess that wasn't yours and made it your own."

"Wouldn't you do the same for your brothers?" I turn the tables on him.

"Where is Mira now?"

I swallow. Good question. I wish I could answer him.

"Megan?" His voice gets hard. "Where is she?"

"She's safe," I say confidently. "So long as the payments keep being made, she'll stay safe. Marco says he can find her if he wants to. You guys seem to have a lot of resources behind you."

His left eyebrow arches.

"Don't put me in the same group as that bastard." He's offended?

The man has me pinned to a wall in his torture chamber!

"Alexander, I have to go home. I have to find some way to get Marco to give me an extension, and I have to beg for my job back if I've lost it." I pause. "Because of you!"

He shakes his head.

"Yes, you! If you would have just left me alone, this wouldn't be happening."

"I'm not leaving you alone, and I'm sure as hell not letting you meet up with Marco to discuss anything." He pushes off the wall and takes two steps back. "I'll take care of Marco."

"Take care of him how?" Not that the world would be

worse off if Marco wasn't in it, but I don't want to be responsible for a bunch of gangsters opening fire on each other in the streets. Too many innocent people could get hurt.

"That's not your concern."

"Then I'll owe the money to you?"

It's just a number in a new ledger, if I let him do this. I'm not any freer. Mira won't be any safer. If she would just get in touch with me, we could figure out what to do next.

"There's a bigger problem at hand," he says.

"What are you talking about?"

"Dexter Thompson was murdered. And whoever sent you to get that drive is most likely behind it."

I shake my head. "I don't want to know. I'm not involved in any of that."

"Oh, but you are, Megan." He steps forward. "Until we find out exactly who did it and why, you're in danger."

"Why would I be in danger?" So long as Marco gets his money, I'm safe from him. Mira can stay safe.

"Because you didn't get the drive to them. And you're the only link to them that's still alive, that we know of."

My heart slams into my ribs. "So, you think they'll come after me?"

"You're definitely a loose end." He nods.

"So, you're not going to let me go home?" I glance at the door. There's still no hope of me getting out of here without his approval.

"No, Megan." He steps in front of me, blocking me again. "I'm not letting you go home."

The back of his knuckles runs along my cheekbone. "And if you try to run again, this will be your new room."

There's a chill to his tone, just cold enough for me to know he means what he says. Alexander doesn't make idle threats.

"All right," I say as though I have some choice in this. "But my job."

He closes his eyes as though he needs a moment to calm himself.

"Your only job right now is to go back up to our room and rest that ankle. It's still bothering you. I can tell."

"Our room?"

"Yes." He nods.

"But you weren't— You haven't been sleeping in there, have you?" Every night I was alone and when I woke up, I was alone.

He cocks a grin.

"No, I haven't been. But that changes tonight." He makes a point of looking me over. "Now that I know you're feeling better."

"But..."

"We can talk over the terms of your new loan then."

Fourteen

Megan

"You'll never get that door open." A soft voice scares me into dropping the hairpin I have shoved into the lock of Alexander's office door.

Spinning around, I find a woman, a little younger than me, leaning against the wall with her arms folded and her glossy pink lips pulled into a knowing grin. She gives a pointed look at the hairpin lying on the carpet at my feet.

"Do you really think a man like Alexander Volkov is going to have a lock that can be picked with a bobby pin?" She bends down and scoops it up, pocketing it in the front pocket of her jeans.

I blink a few times, then look down the hall, half expecting him to come storming toward us.

"He's not home if that's what you're worried about," she says.

"I didn't think anyone was home," I say.

"Just the staff and me." She tilts her head a little to the left. "But I'm not supposed to be here, so we'll say I'm not." She winks.

I blink a few more times. Maybe she's a conjuring of my imagination. I'd been thinking, since Alexander left this morning—after giving me another warning about trying to leave—that this house is too big to be all alone in it.

"Do you live here?" I ask, suddenly very aware that a man like Alexander probably isn't single. Mortification heats my skin.

"No. Not really." Her perfectly sculpted eyebrows pull together. "Oh God, oh no!" She bursts out laughing. "Alexander is my brother! I'm not his... Oh, I can see what you're thinking."

She falls forward a step and holds on to my arm, still laughing.

"His sister?" Of course.

"You should have seen your face." She sobers up a little and smiles.

"I'm sorry. You just surprised me, is all. I didn't realize Alexander had a sister."

"I'm not talked about much." Her smile fades a little at the edges. "The bastard daughter." She rolls her eyes. "We share a father, but not a mother."

Oh.

"And you? Why are you trying to break into his office?" She lifts her chin in the direction of the door that refuses to open.

"I think my cell phone is inside," I say plainly. I've searched my bag, my purse, and both bedrooms I've been in, and the phone is gone. If my math is right, Mira is due to send me a message. She hasn't in the last month and a half, but I need to check my phone to be sure.

"And why would he lock your phone inside his office?" She looks like she's thoroughly enjoying my discomfort.

I sigh.

"Because your brother can be a real asshole," I state

matter-of-factly. "He's keeping me here against my will and all I want to do is call a friend and my boss. Definitely my boss." Maybe if I come up with a good enough story as to why I just haven't shown up the past few days, he'll let me keep my job.

She stares at me for a beat, her face going stoic.

I've just insulted her brother.

"He can be an asshole." She nods. "A huge one, in fact."

Relief floods me.

"Will you help me?" Hope balloons inside me.

"Sorry." She grimaces. "If I did, he'd have my ass."

"Damn right, I would." Alexander comes around the corner, his expression tense. "Elana, what are you doing here?"

"See?" She scrunches her face, then turns to him. "Not exactly the words of a loving brother."

He lifts an eyebrow. "You know what I mean. It's late and you have classes in the morning."

"I know it's hard for your old brain to understand, but there's internet almost everywhere now, so I don't have to stay tethered to my apartment in order to keep up with my classes." She rolls her eyes. "Why are you keeping this girl locked up here?"

He sighs.

"Because," he answers in a flat tone, which I've come to realize means he's not going to say another word about it.

"Well, she'd like her phone back." She jerks her thumb at me, and my face instantly reddening with a blush.

"Would she?" He glances over his sister's shoulder at me, a hint of a smile tugging at the corner of his lips. "Is that why you're standing at my office door?"

"I was just seeing if you were inside," I quickly say before Elana can rat me out.

"She was knocking really loud; that's how I heard her over here," she says in an attempt to help me.

"Really?" His left eyebrow arches higher. "So the scratches on the handle aren't from someone trying to pick the lock?"

"Did you have dinner yet?" sshe counters his question. "I think we should have a late dinner. Maybe Cornelia left something in the kitchen we can warm up."

Alexander puts his hand up to stop her.

"We ate. Go find yourself some food. I need to deal with something."

"It's me. I'm the something." I lift my hand a little and Elana grins.

Alexander makes a low sound in his chest that gets Elana's attention.

"I'm going." She rolls her eyes at him, then points two fingers at me. "I'll see you tomorrow."

"Maybe." Alexander takes a step between us, blocking her from my view. "We'll see how the next hour goes."

I'm not sure what comes over me, but I pinch his back after he makes that statement.

His body locks up the moment I do it, and I jerk back. What the hell did I do?

"Good night, Elana," he says with such finality, my throat dries. She doesn't say another word. I can only hear her soft steps as she heads away from us.

There's no possibility of being saved now.

He's going to kill me.

As he turns around to face me, his icy stare hits me, and I retreat a step.

"Did you just pinch me?" He tilts his head a little, which only exasperates the severity of his frown.

"I did." Showing him fear will only work against me.

He frowns for a moment and shakes his head.

"My sister's already being a bad influence on you." He pulls a set of keys from his pants pocket and unlocks the door, pushing it open. "After you."

I step inside, trying to put as much space between us as possible, as if he's going to snatch me up any second. Which is ridiculous because he's already holding me prisoner in his enormous home.

The door shuts behind me and he walks around me to his desk.

Like every other room in this place, his office is immaculate and perfectly designed to suit him. All the woodworking is dark mahogany with dark-blue hues in the rugs and drapery coverings. The dark leather couches face each other with a glass-topped table between them.

A silver-plated skull sits in the center of the table. It's been fitted onto a platform and transformed into a vase. Bloodred roses spring from the scalp.

What an odd item to have as a centerpiece.

"Is that... real?" I point to the makeshift vase.

He follows my finger. "Yes."

My stomach falls an inch with his answer.

"It's a real skull? It belonged to someone and now you use it to hold flowers?"

"It belonged to a man who betrayed my father," he says casually. That bombshell just hangs between us.

"Are you serious?" I need to double my efforts to get away from this man.

Maybe he's just messing with me, to make sure I understand how serious he is. He wants me to fear crossing him. That's all.

"I am." He walks to the flowers and gently runs his hands over the tops. "My father brought this with him when he immigrated here from Russia. He had it preserved and designed it into a vase."

I nod as if I understand, but the only thing to understand is his father was crazy. And from what I've experienced with Alexander so far, I'm not sure the apple ever left the tree.

"You wanted your phone." He shifts his stance so he's blocking the skull from my view. "Why?"

It takes a second for me to catch up to the change in topic. This man keeps an enemy's skull in his office; what sort of chance do I have of ever getting away from him?

"I need to call work. If I still have a job, I need to tell them something. I can't just not show up," I say once my brain is fully functional again.

"I've already taken care of your job." He shrugs like it's no big deal.

"What does that mean, you took care of it?"

"It means, I took care of it. You don't have to worry about a job."

I take a small step forward.

"I don't have to worry about a job? Meaning, you what...? Did you tell them I wasn't coming back?" I need that job. It's not the best paying but it's good experience. I'll be able to get a better paid position in a year or two.

"You're not going back," he says so matter-of-factly, it almost sounds normal.

"Are you crazy?" I yell. "You can't just quit my job for me! I need my job! It's MY job!" I'm still yelling because he's finally made me snap.

"Megan, lower your voice," he orders softly. "I let you get away with the pinch, but I won't allow you yelling like a spoiled brat."

"Spoiled brat?" I suddenly wish I had the skull in my hands so I could throw it at his head. "How can I be a spoiled brat when you've kidnapped me, locked me up, beaten me, and now you took away the only source of income

I had?" My voice isn't coming down on its own; my blood is too hot.

His eyes narrow slightly and he remains silent.

It's worse when he's quiet. I can tell he's thinking about what he wants to do to me.

"I didn't beat you," he finally says.

"That's what you got out of what I just said?"

"I didn't beat you. I punished you, and I'll do it again when it's needed. And if you don't stop yelling, it will be."

I take a deep breath as I take a small step back. "I needed that job, Alexander." I force my voice to lower.

"Not now, you don't."

It's like throwing a tennis ball at a wall; everything I say just bounces right off him and comes barreling back at me.

"But why? Why don't I need the job?" Even if the debt to Marco magically gets wiped away, rent is still a thing.

"Because."

My muscles tighten with his answer. Anger curls my toes in my shoes.

"Because why?"

He tilts his head a little and a ghost of a smile haunts his mouth. "Because I said."

This man is going to give me a stroke with the speed in which he pisses me off.

"You can't just say that. I want to know why."

"All you need to know is that for the foreseeable future, I'm taking care of you."

My eyelid twitches. This conversation isn't going anywhere and since I'm not physically able to get out of this mansion-prison, I suppose fighting about a job can wait.

"Fine. I need to call Billy to see if those men came back." After I check for Mira's message, I should ask Billy to check my mail. Maybe she mailed me something from wherever she's hiding.

"They haven't. I have men at your building in case they do, so you don't need to call Billy."

"I still want to talk to him." Need. This is a definite need.

"Why?"

"Because." There. Two can play the game of simply making a statement and letting it lie there. See how he likes having it played on him.

"That's not an answer."

"It seems to be when you say it," I mutter.

Great. Now he's making me sound like a brat.

I thrust my hand forward. "I just want my phone. And it's mine, so give it to me."

He stares at it for a moment, then lifts his eyes to mine.

"No."

"Why?"

"Because."

This man wants me to lose my mind, that's what his game is. If I go crazy, then he can easily kill me without any sort of remorse.

Not that he would have an iota of remorse anyway. The man has a skull on his table!

"I don't trust you." He pulls out his own phone and swipes across the screen until he finds what he wants, then turns it to me.

My heart skids to a halt.

"You lied to me, Megan. Again, you lied."

Fifteen

Megan

A profile picture of Detective James Calloway stares at me from Alexander's phone.

"Do you know this man?" While still holding the phone so I can see the screen, he swipes his middle finger across the screen. "And before you lie to me again, I want you to think real hard."

The second photograph is of the detective stepping out of my apartment building.

"Uh." Thoughts, explanations for why that man would be in my building fly through my mind.

Just because he was in my building doesn't mean he was there to see me. He could have been at anyone's apartment.

"That's it?" He puts the phone away and folds his arms over his chest.

"What do you want me to say, Alexander?"

"The truth." He takes a predatory step in my direction. "Let's try that for once, Megan. I'm tired of your lies. You tell me one more and you'll spend the night in the pit."

My throat closes around that threat. I have no doubt he

means the room with the meat hook and he'll put me there and leave me.

"If you would just leave me alone, you wouldn't need to know anything." Every step I take backward, he matches until I hit the couch and fall onto the thick cushions.

Taking the opportunity, he leans over me, completely caging me in.

"I'm not going to leave you alone, Megan. Now tell me the truth. Why would a detective be at your apartment? And who sent you to get the drive on Dexter Thompson?"

We're back to that now?

I stare up at him, at the fierceness in his eyes, the tight lock of his jaw. How did I think I could lie to him and get away with it?

"You didn't find out when you went digging into my life?" I question him back. If he's so powerful, how does he not already know?

"You're going to tell me. I would like to know that you are at least capable of the truth."

"I only lied to protect Mira," I argue. Obviously, I'm not skilled in it.

"Tell me," he orders as he reaches down and begins to unbutton my shirt. I grab at the ends, but he slaps my hand. "Talk."

"What are you doing?"

"Preparing you." He keeps unbuttoning the shirt until it's all the way open.

"For what?"

"You're not talking yet. Would you rather have this conversation in the pit?"

I hate the way he says that, like it's a fun place for him to be. Maybe for him it is. He's not the one who would be hanging from the metal hook like a side of beef.

"Please. Just let me deal with this on my own."

His fingers trail along my collarbone.

"Why? What sort of trouble have you gotten yourself into? Tell me." It's the way his voice softens at the end that breaks my resolve. "I can't fix it for you if I don't know what it is."

Tears threaten but I blink them back while turning away from him. The last six months have been nothing but stress and pressure, and here is man who could probably fix the whole thing if I just tell him.

But if I let him in, he could make things worse. It's a gamble, trusting him. It's a bigger gamble trusting myself around him. With his touch alone, he can set my soul ablaze. No matter the danger rolling off him, something inside my core says to tell him. To give over and trust him. But what if I'm wrong?

"Megan." He cups my chin gently, drawing me back to him. "What is it?"

His brow is pulled together and there's more than frustration now; there's legitimate concern. I could be wrong, but what if I'm not?

I draw in a shaky breath.

"He wasn't there to talk to me. He was there looking for Mira." The words scratch my throat as they leave me. I've been holding back the truth of the nightmare for so long, it hurts to give it life.

"What about her? She moved away months ago." Of course he would think that, but I doubt any sort of financial records he dug up would tell him why.

"She did. She had to." I swallow. "Nico, that was her boyfriend at the time. He was doing stupid stuff. He started dealing for the DeAngelo family, but he messed up."

Alexander's hand drops from my chin. "He was a dealer?"

"Yes. But something happened. I'm not sure if he lost the

drugs or they were stolen, but whatever it was, he ended up being short on the money he owed Marco. By a lot."

"How much?"

I shake my head a little. "I don't know for sure. But Nico couldn't pay him and Marco—" I pause. "Marco blamed him and Mira for it. He killed Nico—right in front of her. He only let her go because she promised to get the money for him."

"She was dealing too?"

"No! She would never do that. But Marco didn't care about that. He just wanted his money."

"How does Calloway play into this?"

"Nico's body was found a few weeks later and the police started investigating. They tried talking to Mira, but she didn't tell them anything." I harden my voice as best I can. "And when she continued telling them nothing, that detective picked her up and brought her into the police department. Marco got wind of it. He didn't believe her when she told him she hadn't said a word."

"The detective brought her in knowing Marco would get the information."

"That's what I thought, yeah. So, after some discussion, Mira and I decided she should leave town. Marco didn't just want the money, he wanted her. She needed to get away before that happened."

"And now Marco is coming after you?" His voice hardens like he's angry at Mira.

"Yes. When the cops didn't go after Marco, we thought he let it go. But the detective kept coming around, kept wanting to talk to Mira. It was too dangerous for her to stay."

"If she lies as horribly as you do, he probably figured she was hiding the truth," he butts in.

"Of course I'm horrible at it; this is my first time having to deal with the mafia. I wasn't raised to lie and steal and kill!"

"Tell me more about Mira." He skips over the accusation of him being a murderer, probably because he's murdered people and can't defend the accusation.

"She wanted to stay, but I insisted she leave town so the detective couldn't get to her and Marco might drop it. She had no idea Marco would come after me."

He pinches the bridge of his nose and takes a slow breath.

"Have you talked with her since she left? Where is she now?"

"I don't know where she is. At first, she'd gone to stay with a friend from high school. But after Marco showed up at our apartment the first time, we figured it was better if I didn't know where she was."

His jaw keeps tightening as I talk, but he remains silent, letting me get through it.

"She left her friend's place and didn't tell either of us where she was going. She's been sending money. Every month she sends two thousand dollars so I can pay Marco for her. As long as he gets his money, he won't chase her. But if he doesn't..." Both of us are on the hook.

"But she stopped sending the money. That's why you missed the payment last month?"

"Yeah. She's supposed to check in every other week, but six weeks ago, she stopped. The next payment she sent was only half the usual amount, and then the money stopped altogether. I have no idea where she is or if she's okay."

"And you're sure Marco hasn't gone looking for her?"

"I'm not sure of anything." I sink back into the couch, wishing it would just suck me in and transfer me to some other dimension where none of this was happening.

Six months of worry and stress bubble in my chest. The tears I've been fighting back for months finally win and slip down my cheeks.

Alexander wipes them away with his thumbs.

"How does the flash drive play into all of this?" he questions softly.

"Marco asked me to get the drive. He said if I was able to get the drive, then Mira's debt would be paid." I take a shaky breath. "Then she could come home and things would be normal again."

He sighs, probably because of how naive I've been. Nothing will be normal again.

Nico is dead.

Mira's been in hiding for months.

And I've been kidnapped by the Volkov family.

"You should have told me this at the start." He leans in as he wipes the rest of the tears from my cheeks.

"The first time I met you, you bent me over a desk and spanked me! Then you showed up in my apartment in the middle of the night."

"If you had told me, I could have helped."

I grab his wrist and stare up at his eyes.

"Helped? You threw me in your trunk. You hunted me through the woods. Literally hunted, with a gun! Why would any of that make me think you would help and not make it worse?"

He shifts his gaze to where my hand has his wrist captured. It's not like he can't just take his arm back, but that's not how Alexander works. He can take, but he'd rather I give.

"You may not be the Italian mob, but you're still mafia," I whisper, releasing his wrist.

He stands up to his full height and stares down at me for a beat before he turns to go to his desk. It's only a moment, but even a moment pinned by his focused gaze slows time.

When he comes back, my cell phone is cradled in his palm.

"Check for her message." He hands it to me.

I'm not looking a gift mobster in the mouth, so I grab it and immediately scroll the notifications.

There are a few texts from the girls at work,, wondering what happened and why I quit.

I didn't quit, but I'll deal with that later.

There is nothing from Mira, so I open my email app. Other than junk emails, there's nothing.

The heaviness returns to my chest.

"Nothing. She's supposed to send proof of life every other week." I pull up the messaging app and open her last message. "She doesn't use her phone, so the number is always different. But I know it's her because she uses the little black heart emoji."

He takes the phone back from me and looks over her last text.

"And this last message was like the others?"

"Yeah. Well, for the most part. I usually send her back a message letting her know things on my end are okay, and she responds, but she didn't respond last time."

He starts scrolling through my messages, probably finding all the ones with that emoji.

"This last one was different. Shorter than the others."

"I just figured she was busy or something. But now... maybe Marco got a hold of her."

"When you only made half the payment last month, what did he say? Did he mention her?"

"Yes. He said if I didn't have that half plus this month's, then he'd have to start turning over rocks to find her. Or something like that, he's not very articulate." He gets his message across just fine, though. I've never not understood our lives were at stake.

"Do you have a picture of her on your phone?" He taps the

screen and starts scrolling through the camera roll. He turns the phone to me after he finds something. "This her?"

It's a picture of Mira and me at a retirement party for one of the guys at work.

"Yeah. Her hair's probably longer now, if she didn't cut it. That picture was taken last April. Just before it all happened."

"And that's Nico?" He points to Mira's boyfriend sitting in the background of the photo.

"That's him." I nod. I reach for my phone when he starts swiping and tapping away. "What are you doing?"

"I'm sending the pictures to my phone."

"Why?"

"Because." He takes the phone back to his desk and puts it away in the top drawer. I suppose it doesn't matter if I know where it is; it's not like I can get into this room without his key.

"Now." He comes back to the couch, leaning over and grabbing my chin. His eyes have darkened. The glimpse of a man who might actually sympathize with my situation is long gone.

Alexander the mobster is back.

"The drive. What did Marco say about the drive? Tell me everything, Megan. No more hiding things or lying."

"Marco gave me that paper I showed you and told me to call the number on it. When I did, the person who answered told me how to get into your office at the club and where the box you kept all your blackmail stuff would probably be."

His grip tightens.

"Who was he?"

"I don't know." I wince when his fingers dig into my chin. "Really, Alexander. I swear, I don't know. He never said who he was, only what to look for and where. He said he'd contact me for the drop-off later."

He stares at me for a moment.

"I'm telling you the truth, Alexander. Marco wanted the drive."

His nose brushes against mine as he makes a low guttural sound.

"If you ever lie to me again, Megan, even a tiny fib, I will punish you so severely, you'll wish I'd hung you up on the hook." He sinks his hand into my hair, pulling my head back. "Tell me you understand. Swear you're done lying."

"I understand," I say quickly. "I promise. No more lies."

"Good." He releases me and walks back to his desk, leaving me sitting on the couch with my blouse open to the cool air of the room.

He walks around his desk, slides off his suit jacket, and tosses it over the back of his chair before sinking into it. The silence grows. I start to button my blouse.

"Come here." He points to the front of his desk. "Stand in front of me."

There's a shift in his tone; he's not interrogating anymore. No, this man I've seen already.

"Take off your clothes." He gestures to me once I'm standing where he wants me. "I want to see what my protection and my money have gotten me."

Sixteen

MEGAN

A shiver crawls through my spine at the firmness of his tone. His harsh gaze falls on me and holds me rooted to the spot.

After a moment passes and I'm still frozen before him, his left eyebrow slowly lifts into a sharp peak. He's already touched me in the most private places. Hell, we've already fucked. But the way he's looking at me, like he wants to take stock, paralyzes me.

"Megan." My name breaks through the silence. "Now is not a good time to rebel against me. Take. Off. Your. Clothes."

There are two buttons left on my blouse to work open, then I'm able to shrug out of the blouse. After draping it across the chair beside me, I shimmy out of my jeans and add them to the chair.

I glance at him with some hope that he'll let me stop here.

He tilts his head in a silent question—*Why aren't you doing as told?*

Focusing my attention on the task at hand, I move my gaze

to the black stapler. It seems so out of place. An ordinary, run-of-the-mill stapler sitting among such extravagance, it's not supposed to be here.

Like me.

The hook of my bra comes undone easily and the straps fall down my shoulders. I grab the cups before they can drop away from my chest. He's seen me already—there's nothing I can hide from him—yet self-preservation rules me.

There's no point; he'll take it from me if he wants to. He can rip off my panties and do whatever he wants to me. No one here will stop him.

I pull the bra free of my arms and drop it with the rest of my clothes, then hook my thumbs into the elastic of my panties. Shoving them down over my hips and down to my ankles, I busy my mind, blocking out the fact that he's watching.

Judging.

"Put your hands on your head," he orders, leaning back in his chair like a king.

"Alexander, what are you doing? I'm sorry I lied." I fold my arms over my chest and press my thighs together as tightly as I can.

"I'm sure you are. Especially since you got caught." He moves to his feet effortlessly and glides around the desk, never taking his heated gaze off me.

When he's behind me, the warmth of his body spreads across my bare back. He leans into me, the soft dusting of his five o'clock shadow rough against my shoulder.

"Hands on your head. I'm tired of fighting you. You're going to learn once and for all who is in charge here." His voice is firm, raw, unwavering.

Raising my hands over my head, I lay them one on top of

the other. My nipples pull tight as my face erupts into an inferno.

"See, not so difficult." He kisses my shoulder as his arms wrap around my middle. His touch is light, feathering upward to my breasts.

My breath catches as he takes both nipples between his fingers and pinches. When he releases me, he kisses my neck.

"You need to be punished." He drags his teeth along the soft flesh of my neck.

"No, I don't." A mouse makes more noise than me at this point. It's his fault for all his leather and spice smell, his heated body next to me, and his fingers still trailing along my body, outlining me.

"You do." He grabs my hips and spins me around to face him, lifting me at the same time and hoisting me onto his desk. The stapler and other desk items are knocked out of the way as he pushes me farther onto the desk.

I catch his gaze; the simmering chocolate of his eyes heats me to my core. It shouldn't be so easy for him to get into my head. Just a look, a simple touch, and I'm melting for him.

It's not fair.

Using both hands, he pushes my hair from my face. "No more lying."

"I already promised."

"Say it again," he orders roughly.

"I promise. No more lying."

"Unbuckle my belt." He grabs my wrists and puts them at his waist. If he wasn't staring down at me with such severity, maybe I'd be able to tell him to go to hell a little easier.

Pulling the thick leather through the loop of his trousers and then working it through the buckle, a flood of warmth settles deep inside of me. Was this the belt he put around my neck the other night? It feels heavy, as that one did, but I'm sure a man like Alexander has more than one belt.

"Now undo my pants." He brushes another hair away when it falls forward. The button opens easily, and I grasp the zipper.

A pang of unease cuts through the heat pooling low in my core. If I refuse him, what will happen to me, to Mira? Is this the price for his protection... to become his plaything, to sell myself to him? It feels like an invisible collar around my throat. And worse, I can't decide if I hate it or crave it.

"Megan." My answer is in the way he says my name. It's softer, sensual.

When I tilt my eyes up to his, I instantly lose myself in the molten chocolate of his gaze. He won't take more than I'm willing to give. And in this moment, I seem more willing than ever to give over to him completely.

He steps closer, enveloping me in the masculine scent of his aftershave and the warmth of his body, allowing me to undo his zipper with more ease. The room is silent, save for the teeth of the zipper opening.

"Good girl. Reach in and pull out my cock," he whispers into my ear, sending a tremor through my body.

He steps even closer, making it easier to slip my hand into the opening of his trousers. Sliding my hand beneath the elastic of his black boxers, the tips of my fingers brush against him.

His breath catches as I glide my hand along the thick length of him and wrap my hand around the base of his cock. It's so warm and solid, so fucking hard. With my free hand, I shove his trousers and boxers down enough for his cock to spring free.

"Good girl." He wraps his hand around the back of my

neck, drawing me up to him, and kisses me. It's a harsh kiss, one screaming of possession.

When he breaks the kiss, he spreads my legs open, wraps his arm around my waist, and pulls me to the edge of the desk.

Slowly, I stroke his cock, feeling the strength of him in my palm. I squeeze a little, determined to show him he's not the only one with power.

He lets loose a guttural sound and shoves my hand away. He sweeps my right leg up and cradles it in his elbow while he drives forward in one thrust.

I have to lean back a little as his cock fills me, stretches me. He gives me no time to adjust to his size as he thrusts into me again and again, pulling me closer to him with each thrust.

Grabbing on to the edge of the desk, I use it as an anchor as his thrusts get harder. My ass edges across the desk with each movement.

"Look at me, Megan," he demands and my gaze flicks to his. His brow pulls tight as he drives into me. "Lean back," he orders, sliding his hand from behind my neck and slowing his movements.

Dropping my elbows to the desk, I lower my back to the desk while one hand grips my hips, pulling me toward him as he plows into me.

"Such a good girl now. Play with yourself for me. Play with that little clit of yours." His fingertips dig into my thigh as he gives his order. "I want to see you play."

Hunger like I've never felt before creeps up into my soul. I want his approval here. No, I need it.

I need him to call me his good girl again.

Slowly, I reach between our bodies. His eyes never leave my movements as the tips of my fingers brush across my sensitive, swollen clit.

"Fuck," I whisper as the sensations build.

He scrapes his teeth over his bottom lip while watching me play with my clit for him. At his command. His jawline tenses and he thrusts even harder.

Reaching even farther down, my fingers graze his shaft as he plows in and out of my pussy. He groans as I split my fingers around his cock, rubbing it as he continues to fuck me.

"Your clit," he growls, twisting his hips and hitting a spot inside me that erupts into a shower of pleasure.

I slide a second hand between our bodies and begin to roll my clit beneath the tip of my middle finger. I'm no stranger to this and I know exactly where the pressure point is. It's no time before I'm teetering at the edge.

"Fuck," he grunts as my eyes roll back and the sensations pull me to the very brink.

How can a man who makes me see red just by being in the room give such pleasure? It's as though his touch can wash away all the irritation, all the arrogance, all the fucked-up messes of everything around me.

I pull my free leg back, resting the heel on the edge of the desk, and arch upward to him. I'm so fucking close. Every muscle tightens, and the coil is ready to spring.

"Oh!" The pleasure crests. I'm about to free-fall over the edge into oblivion. One more—

"No, no." Alexander grabs my wrist, pulling my touch away from my body just as the first wave of my orgasm was about to sweep me away.

"No!" I tug on my hand, but he has that cocky grin on his face again.

When I move my other hand, he releases my leg and grabs hold of my wrist as well. Easily, he captures both wrists in one hand as he pulls free of my body and fists his own cock.

He strokes himself, rubbing the tip of his dick over my

pussy lips as he finds his own release, leaving me dangling over the edge.

"Alexander!" I moan. It's not fair.

Hot ropes of cum land on my pussy and just above, some getting on my stomach. His eyes close and he draws in a deep breath, letting my wrists go.

When he opens them, the warm pool of arousal is gone, and the stone is back.

"Naughty girls don't get to come, Megan." He steps back from the desk and tugs his clothes back on, tucking his cock, still slick with my arousal, into his boxers.

I swallow around the rage building in my throat and scramble from the desk. How do I keep letting him put me in these situations? He just used me! He fucking used me like some cheap whore and now he's grinning at me while I stuff myself back into my clothes.

"You... I hate you." I glare at him once I'm dressed.

He nods. "You hate how turned on you are right now."

"No, Alexander. I hate you." I throw my shoe at him, which he easily catches and brings to me.

"You dropped this," he says with that arrogant grin of his that makes my blood boil.

I sigh. There's no winning here.

"I'm tired. I just want to go to bed." I snag the shoe from him and carry both of them to the door.

"It is late," he agrees, joining me at the door and opening it.

When we get to the bedroom, I go straight to the bathroom to wash off the mess he'd left on my body with a warm washcloth. Most of it soaked into my clothes, but there's a remnant of his cum clinging to my skin.

After scrubbing off the evidence of my punishment, I dump everything into the laundry and throw on my nightshirt.

Surely he has to be gone by now, so I venture out into the bedroom. Disappointment mixed with relief fills me at the sight of the empty room.

I slip beneath the covers, glancing at the door.

He didn't even say good night.

The closet door opens, and he walks out in his boxers, working open the band of his watch.

"What are you doing?" I ask as he casually walks around the foot of the bed. "You didn't mean it when you said you were staying in here tonight."

His shirt is gone, leaving me with the view of his muscular chest and stomach. I knew he was fit, but fuck, the man is solid. The ripples of his stomach fade into a distinctive V-shape, leading my eye to the elastic of his boxers.

My body still craves an ending he refused me, and seeing him in this state is making my situation worse. I need him to leave, so I can fix this.

But instead of heading to the door, he pulls back the covers on the other side of the bed.

"Of course I did. I don't say things I don't mean." He climbs in and brings the blankets up over himself as he leans up on his elbow to look at me.

"Maybe I should go to a different room then?"

"You're not going anywhere." He brushes his fingertips along my jaw. "Go to sleep. If you're a good girl, maybe I'll reward you in the morning."

I clench my jaw and flip over to my right side. Fine. If he wants to sleep here, fine. It's his bed after all. And it's enormous.

There's no reason we can't both be in it and not even touch.

The lights go out and a second later, his heavy arm wraps

around my middle and I'm dragged halfway across the bed until his chest is pressed against my back.

"I hate you," I whisper into the dark.

"I know." He pushes the hair from my neck and places a soft kiss.

"You can't keep me here forever."

He presses one more kiss.

"Can't I?"

SEVENTEEN

ALEXANDER

Steam billows around Megan as she saunters out of the bathroom wrapped in a towel. Beads of water still cling to her shoulders and legs.

The moment she sees me, she freezes.

"I thought you were gone for the day." She grabs on to the edge of the towel, tucking it farther in and securing it. If she thinks a little bit of fabric is going to keep me from taking what I want from her, she hasn't been paying any attention.

"Not yet." I lean my hip against the dresser, watching her. I spent a good amount of time last night watching her sleep. She was adorable wrapped up in all the blankets, tucking everything up to her chin as though it could ward me off.

Once I fell asleep though, it was a deep sleep. I haven't slept that good in years. Something which caught me off guard when I woke this morning. I felt completely at ease.

"What do you want?" she demands when I keep silent.

"That's a lot of attitude for first thing in the morning." I push off the dresser and stalk toward her. She tightens her hold on the towel. "Did you touch yourself this morning?"

Her jaw drops at my question.

"Isn't that why you were so upset about me staying with you last night? Because you wanted to take what I wouldn't give you?" I stop advancing only when the toes of my shoes brush against her bare feet.

"No." She flings the answer at me like a headstrong brat who's being called out.

"Remember, no more lies." I try to harden my expression, but she's gone and tucked her lip between her teeth.

"Did you pleasure yourself in the shower?" I ask again when she goes silent. It's better, I suppose, than outright lying.

"No." She gives a little shake of her head, and water droplets fly from the ends of her hair.

"Did you want to?" I slide my hands into my pockets, letting her think she's safe from me. At least for the moment.

"Don't you have somewhere to be? I know I do, but you won't let me go." She narrows her pretty eyes at me.

"I'm always exactly where I want to be, Megan. Now, answer me."

"I'm not answering that." She shoves past me, an attempt at dismissing me.

"Hmm, then I think I have my answer."

"I need to get dressed; can you go lurk somewhere else?" She tries to wave me off, but I won't be turned away. Not in my own house, in my own bedroom. Not going to happen.

With quiet, deliberate steps, I make my way across the bedroom to her. She's standing behind the bed, as though anything could get in my way when I want something. Her eyes never leave me as I stalk toward her. The grip on her towel increases.

When I get to her, she tries to take another step back, but there's nowhere left for her to go. She's turned to face me, the bed at her back.

And that fucking towel is still wrapped around her damn body.

"You're grouchy this morning." I run the back of my knuckles across her jaw. "Are you always like this when you wake up?"

"When I wake up still a prisoner, yes." She gives a hard enough nod that small water droplets fly onto my shirt.

"A prisoner of your own doing." I trail my fingertips over her shoulder, down her bare arm, leaving little goose pimples on her silky skin in my wake.

"I've told you everything." Her voice softens. "I swear, Alexander. I don't have any other information for you."

I move my gaze from her flesh to her pretty azure eyes that she tries so hard to keep stoic. It never works; I can see through them.

"I know," I assure her. I inhale the scent of my soap on her skin, enjoying the bit of spice on her. My scent.

"Then you'll let me go?" There's barely any hope in her question.

She's smarter than that, to think I'd let her just waltz out of here after she's told me what's really going on.

I cup her cheek, running my thumb over her bottom lip.

"What do you think?"

"I think you're insane." It's so soft, the little insult, it almost sounds intimate.

"Maybe I am." My brothers will probably think so.

I have the information I need from her. She's not really a threat to us. Whatever danger she's gotten herself into with the DeAngelo family is her problem.

Except it's not. Not anymore.

Brushing her hand away from where the towel is tucked, I grab hold of the material.

"Alexander." She reaches for my wrist. "Don't."

"Don't?" I chuckle as I pull the end of the towel free and unwrap her like a present brought just for me.

Fuck. My breath washes away with the beauty in front of me. She's perfect.

"Alexander." She straightens a little, sucking in her stomach.

"No." I put my hand on her hip. "Don't do that."

Leaning down, I sweep a kiss across her shoulder, then her cheek.

"You're perfect. Never try to be different." I toss the towel to the floor at our feet.

I should walk away, leave her alone. It's what sane man would do. But she's right. I'm insane. And it's all her fault.

Picking her up, I toss her onto the bed. She scrambles back a little until she reaches the headboard.

"What are you doing?" Her eyes flicker to my belt as I unbuckle.

"No more punishment, not this morning." I shove out of my pants and kick them away, yanking my shirt over my head and tossing it into the pile before I stare down at her.

Her eyes are completely locked on my cock. I've never been so hard for a woman before. It's painful, being this needy for someone.

The bed dips beneath my weight as I climb onto it with her. Those large eyes of hers finally move up to mine. Her pupils have grown so much, only a sliver of the blue remains.

"We shouldn't do this," she says, tilting her head back when I climb over her and bring my mouth just above hers.

"That line was crossed already." I wrap my hand around the back of her neck, pulling her up to my kiss.

Fuck, she tastes too tempting not to devour all of her.

"You have to let me go sometime, Alexander," she demands when I break the kiss.

"I'm fucking Alexander Volkov. I don't *have* to do anything. The sooner you understand that, the sooner you'll stop being angry about how unfair you think all of this is."

Before she can let a smart-ass remark loose, I scoot back and pull her legs until she's flat on her back. Spreading her legs, I settle between them, already smelling the sweet aroma of her arousal.

"Alexander, no, don't." She tries to squeeze her thighs together, to stop me from the gift I want. The woman still doesn't understand. She's not going to get away from me, not from my life and certainly not from this bed.

"If you get in my way, I'll change my mind about punishing you more." I look up the length of her body to her. "Stay out of my way."

"But..."

I chuckle. "Stubborn woman. Should I make you spread yourself for me like I did in the yard?"

A sweet pink blush erupts on her chest, exploding up her neck and over her cheeks. Fuck. How can a woman like her have this much innocence inside her. It drives me crazy.

Using my thumbs, I open her pussy lips, exposing the sweet, wet, pink flesh there.

"Soaked already, and I haven't even touched you yet." I smile up at her. "Have you been this needy since last night? Since I left you dangling just above an orgasm I never allowed you to have?"

Her jaw tightens and she raises up onto her elbows, glowering down at me. Even with her pretty thighs spread and my mouth a breath away from her pussy, she tries to argue.

"You don't allow me anything." She tries so hard to say this lie with conviction. It's cute.

"I allow everything when it comes to you. Now be a good girl unless you want to go all day with a needy pussy."

"Your arrogance is astounding. You didn't affect me at all last night."

I'll just have to show her what a liar she is.

I flick her clit with the tip of my tongue. Her thighs tighten, and there's a small gasp.

It's not enough. I want more.

Another flick and she moans.

Still not enough.

Sliding two fingers into her tight, hot passage and she drops her head back. When I bend my knuckles and thrust into her, her arms fall away and she's flat on the bed, her legs opening more for me.

I grin against the warmth of her pussy and increase the pressure of my tongue. Pressing the flat of my tongue against her clit, I lick her, tease her, taste her.

She's so fucking sweet I could feast on her for days.

Her little moans turn into deep, guttural sounds.

"Such a good girl," I mutter against her pussy and the vibration of my words makes her arch her hips up to meet my mouth.

Her thighs tighten around my head, and she bucks up to meet my tongue. I increase the pressure, thrust my fingers harder, twisting them and curling them until her chest heaves with urgency.

She's almost there.

"Good girl. Come for me," I order her, twisting my fingers more, flicking her clit harder.

Faster.

"Be my good girl," I say, and her muscles tremble.

So close.

"My sweet, good girl. Come for me." Her hand dives into my hair, fisting it as she comes unglued.

No burn has ever felt so fucking good.

Her scream is primal as her pussy clenches around my fingers. Moments pass as she comes down from the intensity of her high and I slip my fingers out, licking her arousal from them as I watch her catch her breath.

She starts to turn over, like she's going to get off the bed.

Sweet thing thinks we're done.

Not by a long shot.

Grabbing her hips, I push them back into the mattress and blanket her body with mine.

I intend a soft kiss, but once my lips touch hers, I want all of her. Her lips part slightly, just enough for me to sweep past them and let her taste herself on my tongue.

"Fuck, baby. I need to be inside you." I settle between her legs, the head of my cock pressing against her entrance.

I don't wait for her to nod or speak, I just plow into her body. My eyes roll with the intensity of how good her body feels around me.

"Spread your legs more, baby." I hook my arm under one knee and pull her leg up as I drive into her, chasing a fulfillment I'm not sure will ever come with her.

My balls tighten and I kiss her again and again.

"You're going to come for me again," I say against her lips, slowing my thrusts enough to grind my hips into her. She moans.

"I don't think I can."

I grin down at her.

"It wasn't a suggestion. You are going to come for me again." I slide my hand between our bodies, finding her clit still hard and slick.

Her eyes roll as I tease her clit with the tip of my finger

and continue to drive into her. Leaning down, I take a nipple into my mouth, teasing the tip with my tongue while sucking at the same time.

Another moan, this time deeper.

I thrust harder, needing to be deep inside her. Shifting my position, I let her nipple go, then move to the other, this time taking the bud between my teeth.

"Oh, fuck," she breathes out. Her body tightens beneath me.

"Come, baby. Come hard for me," I order, flicking my tongue over her nipple before lifting up more so I can see her. I want to capture her features when her release takes her away.

"I... oh, fuck... Alexander... oh... God..."

Pulling her leg up an inch more, I drive harder, teasing her clit the whole time.

The waves hit, and the ripples of her orgasm clench my cock as she cries out. Enough is enough, I can't take any more. I thrust harder and faster into her while her orgasm steals her.

Her mouth drops open, her face flush with urgency.

Electric pain zips down my spine as my balls pull tight.

"Fuck," I groan. A flash of light bursts in the periphery of my vision.

It's too much, she's too hot, too wet, too tight.

Too fucking perfect.

My release rips through me and I let out a groan as my jaw clenches.

"Fuck," I moan again when the intensity finally starts to wane. I fall forward, dropping her leg so I can catch myself on my forearms and not crush her with my weight.

I kiss the tip of her nose.

"Oh God! You're not wearing a condom!" Frantically, she wiggles beneath me, pushing at my shoulders. As though leaving the warmth of her body now will change anything.

I kiss her forehead.

"Alexander! I'm not on anything!"

She shoves at me, harder than before, but I barely move.

"I can't believe how stupid I've been!" she snaps.

Stupid? My chest tightens as the meaning of her words sinks in.

"We haven't used protection. Not once."

Her panic slams into me.

Maybe I should regret it, not being careful. But I don't. Deep down, inside the pit of me, the idea of her carrying my child doesn't scare me. It soothes the dark, primal beast inside me.

"Good." I kiss her cheek.

She freezes.

"Good?" It's a question, but it comes out as an accusation.

"Yes." I nod. It's going to take her a little longer to get used to the idea, but I can give her time.

"No."

I nod again.

"Yes."

"Why?" It's almost a whine, like she just can't get a handle on me and it's starting to wear on her.

"Because."

"Because?"

"Yes." I slip from her body, watching my cum slide out from between her pussy lips. It's a thing of beauty.

"You really are insane." She jumps up from the bed as I reach for my clothes.

"I have meetings in the city most of the day. Do you think you can stay out of trouble while I'm gone?" I buckle my belt, leaving my hands on it while I ask the question.

"No. I think I'll burn down the place if you don't let me go home!" She stomps her foot, which makes me chuckle.

"There's enough staff and guards here that I'm not too afraid of that." I adjust the collar of my shirt.

"I hate you."

I smile. "Megan, if that was you hating me,"—I point to the bed—"I never want you to like me."

EIGHTEEN

ALEXANDER

"You got here fast." Ivan meets me in the stairwell leading down to Obsidian.

"You said there's a problem. What is it?" I brush past him and jog down the rest of the stone steps to the secret area beneath our legal moneymaker. It's not that this part of the building is unknown; it's that it's kept off the books.

Things done down here don't belong to the IRS or any other government watchdog agency.

"Did I tear you away from something?" Ivan eyes me. He's only a year younger than me; he knows me better than almost anyone in the world.

"Not something. Someone." Kaz steps out of one of the playrooms just as we pass and joins us.

"What were you doing in there?" I ask, stopping to glance inside.

"Relax. I was checking on the new equipment that arrived." He shakes his head. "I don't dip my pen in the company ink, you know that."

I pause. Kaz has his own set of rules that he follows. He'll break any law that gets in the way of what he wants, but his own rules are strict and ironclad.

"What about the waitress last weekend?" Ivan cocks an eyebrow.

Kaz grins, producing a deep dimple on the left side of his cheek that seems to make the women in this damn city suckers for anything he says after displaying it.

"She worked upstairs." He shrugs. "Different inkwell. Besides, it was her last night. She left to go work at some accounting firm in Joliet. And I thought we were discussing Alexander finally having someone warming his bed long enough that he doesn't want to get up at the ass crack of dawn to work?"

"You stay out of my bed." I push the door to the main office open and we file inside.

"See? She's gotten to him." Kaz walks the periphery of the room before settling himself in the armchair in the corner.

"No one has *gotten* to me." I frown. "She's information, that's all."

"But I thought she's given you all the information you can get from her?" Kaz pushes. He's always the first to find the button that will piss me off the most and press it.

"She's not your concern."

"Oh?" Ivan questions. "She's got ties to DeAngelo, but she's not our concern?"

"She's not a threat to us," I clarify.

"See how his eye gets a little twitchy?" Kaz smirks.

"You're gonna lose your teeth if you keep it up," Ivan says with a pointed finger at our younger brother. "And I'm not gonna stop him."

"Not my fault the man has finally found something other than work to occupy his time and he won't admit it."

Ivan steps in front of Kaz, blocking my view of him.

"You said she's not a threat. But what if DeAngelo is looking for her?"

"Is Rurik here yet?" I'm not going to explain this mess any more times than I have to.

Kaz looks behind me. "Just walked in."

"You are lucky." Rurik strides through the lounge and joins us as the bar. "I was just getting ready to head to the airport when your text came through last night."

"Oh?" I grab a bottle of whiskey and pour him a drink, sliding it across the counter toward him. "Are you in the middle of something?"

He takes the glass. "Nothing that can't wait."

"What's going on exactly?" Kaz leans against the edge of the bar. "Why are you dragging Rurik into this mess if she's no danger to us?"

"Because our friend here is the best hunter I know." I pour myself a drink and throw it back. It does nothing to dull the irritation that my life has turned into since finding Megan standing in the records office wearing that fucking cat mask.

"You're sending Rurik after Marco DeAngelo?" Ivan questions.

"No." I pull out my phone and open the picture of Mira I grabbed from Megan's cell.

"Which one?" Rurik leans over the bar to look at the image. "The black hair with the white stripe or the curly-haired one with the birthmark on her cheek?"

I have to look at the photo again; I hadn't noticed much about Mira other than she wasn't Megan.

"The one with the curls. Her name is Mira Pierce and she's been gone for six months now," I explain and point to Megan's smiling face. "This is Megan, and they've managed to get themselves in trouble with Marco DeAngelo. I have Megan handled, but Mira has been in hiding."

"What did they do?" he asks as I pick up the phone and open the photo, cropping out Megan before sending him the pic.

"They did nothing exactly. Mira's boyfriend, however, was stupid enough to start dealing for Marco. Somehow, he managed to lose his supply and when Marco came for the money, he decided to make an example of him and killed him."

"Fuck," Kaz groans. "And your girl's involved in this shit?"

"No." I shoot him a glare. "She had nothing to do with that, but Mira was there. She saw it. Marco gave her the option of ending up like her boyfriend or getting him the money owed. She opted for a repayment plan."

"But she's been gone for six months." Rurik frowns. "Did she skip town and let your woman take the heat?"

My woman. It's a pleasant sound hearing that from someone other than me.

"The two of them together decided it was safer if she left. There's a detective that has been asking questions and Marco was starting to get suspicious. She's been sending the payments owed while hiding, but the money didn't show up last month or this month, and Megan hasn't heard from her."

"Maybe Marco got her and is just using Megan for the rest of the cash," Ivan points out.

"That's what we need to find out." I look at Rurik. "I have nothing other than her picture, her name, and the place she went when she left town. I went through my usual channels for information, and it's all come up dry."

Rurik rubs his chin, scratching just below his beard.

"I've found people with less. If she's alive, I'll find her. And if she's not." He shrugs. "I'll find that out too."

"What about the money owed to Marco? If she's been paying monthly, he's going to come looking for it soon." Ivan points out.

"We'll deal with him soon enough." The idea of handing over even a penny to that fucking prick makes my stomach turn. We'll need to make him understand it's not her debt, and that anything that was owed to him was paid in full when he took out Nico.

Fuck.

The list of shit to sort through just gets longer by the day, thanks to Megan.

"And if Marco finds Megan before we get this all settled? A debt is a debt, and we'd be doing the same if someone owed." Kaz grabs the whiskey bottle from me and pours another glass for himself. "I know this girl's keeping your bed warm and all but—"

"He touches what's mine and he'll pay for it." My teeth snap together as my jaw tightens. If DeAngelo looks at her, I'll take his fucking eyes.

She's a complication, she's sneaky, and she has an issue with telling the full truth the first time she's asked, but she's my fucking complication and I won't let anyone hurt her.

Ivan studies my face for a moment, then gives a curt nod. "Does she understand that?"

"I haven't explained the full situation yet," I say.

Ivan grins. "Well, good luck with that when you do."

"The bigger issue is Thompson. Marco is the one who sent Megan, but he's not the one who told her where to find the drive and how to get in here. So, we need to find out whose lips have gotten a little loose."

I turn the conversation back to the reason I had to leave Megan naked in my bed. If I didn't have this shit to deal with, I'd still be home waiting for another chance to sink myself into her.

It's not that I haven't had good sex before, but Megan is different. It's not just a fuck with her. It's not enough to just fuck her once or twice. Hell, I'm not sure I'll ever get tired of her.

And that fucking mouth of hers. She has a shyness about her, but once she gets that fire built up in her, she's all molten lava. I can see the fear in her eyes, but she doesn't let that stop her when she has something to say.

And at the moment, it's a lot of anger aimed at me.

I don't blame her, but it will pass.

And then she'll realize she's not going anywhere. That once I've made my claim, it sticks.

She's mine now.

Rurik checks his phone. "I'll check in when I have something. When I find her, what do you want me to do with her?"

"I don't want her hurt. Just bring her home, let her know it's safe. She's probably spooked, and you're not exactly a walking advertisement for a knight in shining armor. It might not be that easy to get her to believe you."

He deadpans, "If you want her home, I'll bring her home." He taps his knuckles on the bar. "You have enough to deal with here. I'll handle this."

"Thank you, my friend. I will owe you." I shake his hand over the bar. Rurik can be counted on without a second of worry. Once he's given his word, it's all but done.

"And I will collect." He flashes a grin, then grabs the bottle of thirty-year-old Glenfiddich whiskey from me and salutes me with it.

"You're letting him take a six-thousand-dollar bottle of whiskey?" Kaz watches Rurik saunter from the club with the bottle.

"At least it wasn't the 1926 Macallan." I shrug. That prized bottle sits in my private office unopened. You don't just casually drink a one-point-six-million-dollar bottle of whiskey.

"If you two can concentrate on something other than

runaway women and expensive liquor, I finally got my hands on the coroner's report for Thompson," Ivan snarks.

"The official one or the real one?" Kaz asks, his levity disappearing. Kaz plays hard, but when it comes to family or our businesses, he's as ruthless as the rest of us.

"Both," Ivan responds. "The official reporting is that he died of a heart attack. But the report we received shows he had potassium cyanide in his blood."

"Cyanide?" Kaz raised his brow. "He was poisoned?"

"The coroner said from the amount of it in his bloodstream, he thinks he was being given small traces of it over time, and whatever he was given the last time was enough to trigger a heart attack," Ivan explains.

"Why wouldn't they want the real cause of death on the certificate?" Kaz leans forward, pressing his elbows into his knees.

"Dexter Thompson was corrupt as fuck. He wasn't just on our payroll. Half the city probably had him in their pocket." The zoning commissioner can keep a developer from getting the land they want and the permits they need to get a project underway. It's easiest to slip him the cash he wants to get your way in new developments.

We don't deal with bribes when not necessary. Every bit of dirt we had on him kept him securely in our pocket.

"Who else knows he was killed?" I ask.

Ivan shrugs. "Anyone who can get to the coroner. We know DeAngelo wanted dirt on Thompson."

"Poison isn't his way." Kaz rubs his temples. "If it was him, he'd have just sent his fucking goons to blow up the man's house."

"The list of who wanted that man dead could be fucking long." If Thompson wasn't doing what someone wanted him to do and they couldn't get him to budge, they could take him out and take the chance on the next commissioner.

"We're supposed to break ground on the resort next month, is that being fucked with?" Kaz questions, his voice hardening.

"Not yet, but the acting commissioner hasn't been announced yet. Our permits are all solid so far, but if they start digging around, wanting to clean up the corruption, it could get messy."

"Until their price is known." I snort. "No politician is incorruptible. They just have pretty titles and the backing of the government."

"So long as we're not being fucked with, it might be best if we wait to see how it plays out," I suggest.

"Yeah. I agree." Kaz gives a solid nod. "The new commissioner might be better for us."

Dexter Thompson's death isn't our problem, so long as whoever steps in is as controllable as he was. If the government wants to hide his murder, that's on them. We have businesses to run.

"Agreed," Ivan says.

"What about the DeAngelo issue and your woman?" Kaz lifts his chin in my direction. "He's not going to walk away just because she's yours now."

"No. He's not," I agree.

"You want company when you meet him?" Ivan offers.

"I'd rather not sit down with the asshole at all, but to make sure the money gets into his hands, and he assures me she's off his radar, I might have to do that." I nod.

"You getting involved could make it messier. Maybe she can just pay him." Kaz has a point.

Stepping in here might give DeAngelo ideas that he can come after us. It could make her a target in order to get to us.

"Would you send your woman into a meeting with DeAngelo?" I question.

He's just as possessive as I am, and when he finds the woman who wakes up the beast inside him, he won't let the poor woman step foot out of his eyesight.

"So, we'll meet him." Kaz nods.

"I'll get a meeting set up." My phone vibrates and I pull it out. One glance at the screen and my jaw tightens.

"What's wrong?" Ivan questions.

"I didn't get a chance to mention yet, but Elana came home last night. She's at the house."

"Doesn't she have school?" Kaz questions.

I shrug. "She's impulsive like always. I don't know what's going on yet. I haven't had a chance to talk to her."

"What's happened?" Ivan questions as I type out a response.

"She's with Megan." I pocket my phone and turn to the door. "And she brought her to a doctor."

"Is she okay?" Kaz asks. "What kind of doctor?"

"She brought her to a gynecologist."

Nineteen

Megan

"Are you sure this is all right?" I question Elana for the third time since we left the house. She reaches across the back seat of the SUV we're being driven in and squeezes my hand.

"Of course it is. You're with me." She smiles. "He never told me I couldn't take you out for lunch."

The emphasis on the word lunch sends the little hairs on my neck standing and I check with the driver to see if he noticed the change in tone.

He doesn't seem to be listening to us at all.

"Going all the way into the city is a long way to go for a sandwich," I point out, looking out the window as the skyscrapers of the city come into view. Now that there's light, and I'm not stuffed into the trunk of a car, I realize where I've been staying. Twenty-five minutes outside of downtown.

Even if I had managed to get myself to a main road the other night, I never would have made it home. Not on foot with the way my ankle was swelling up.

"It's fine," she says again and drops my hand.

"So, you don't go to school here?" I question.

"Oh, I do. I go to Northwestern."

"That's not too far away. You don't like it?"

"Oh, it's fine. I have my own place on campus with some friends." She lifts her shoulder. "It's not the city though, you know. Too far out."

"Yeah." I've never been outside the city other than on short vacations when I was little. One week every summer my parents rented a small cottage on some obscure lake, and we'd just hang out swimming and fishing.

Elana swipes her phone alive and starts tapping away on the screen.

"Is that your brother?" The urge to lean over and see what he might be saying tugs at me, but I manage to keep myself in check.

"No. Just a friend." She grins at the message on her screen, and I get the sense it's not just a friend. After a soft sigh, she types one last message and puts her phone back in the small purse she has strapped across her chest.

The driver flips on his turn signal and we're exiting the expressway. Familiarity relaxes my muscles. I'm almost near my apartment building. If I can get out at the next light, I can grab the bus and in twenty minutes I'd be home.

And then where would I be? Alexander would come looking for me. I'd never be able to hide from him in my neighborhood. Leaving the city is probably the safest thing for me. Away from Alexander and away from Marco. Maybe he'll give up when he realizes I'm gone.

Foolish thoughts, I know.

"You need to relax." Elana taps my leg when the silence stretches between us. "You're with me. We're getting lunch."

"Yeah." I open my purse and pull out my wallet to be sure I still have my insurance card stuffed inside. Without having gone to work in the last few days, I'm sure I'm out of a job, and who knows if the policy is even still going to cover this.

"Just park here, Gregor. We'll walk."

"Elana. I'll pull up to the restaurant," he counters and she sighs.

"Fine. Whatever." She rolls her eyes and sinks back in her seat. I watch as our actual destination passes my window. It's only a block away from the deli Elana lied about us going to, but still, watching it slip away makes me worry.

As soon as the SUV pulls into an open space, Elana jumps out and I reach for the door handle. Gregor groans and mutters something in Russian as I pop open my door and hop down onto the sidewalk.

Elana slips her arm through mine and pulls me toward the door of the deli.

"He's going to park around the corner; let's just wait until he drives off." She keeps her voice down and casually glances back. "Okay, he's gone."

She tugs on me, and we turn just as we reach the door and hurry down the street to the doctor's office we'd passed. By the time we get inside, we're both out of breath and have to give ourselves a minute before hitting the elevator button.

"I need to start working out." I laugh as I hit the number three for the office I need.

"Same." She leans back against the wall of the elevator as it takes us up to the right floor.

The office is bathed in soft lighting and soft-yellow wallpaper. Chairs line the walls. Half of them are filled with pregnant women.

"Hi. You have an appointment?" The receptionist smiles warmly when I step up to the desk. Most doctor's offices I've been in have glass surrounding the reception area, but not here. Everything here is so inviting and warm.

"Hey, Julie." Elana leans her elbow on the desk. "I called about an hour ago and Dr. Simons said he'd squeeze my friend in real quick?"

Julie's eyes warm when she sees Elana.

"Oh, hi. Didn't see you. Sure. I'll let them know you're here."

I pull my purse up onto the desk and grab my wallet.

"I'm a new patient; you'll need my insurance card, right?" I try to hand it to her, but she glances at Elana, then shakes her head.

"No, hun. No need."

"Oh. Forms?" I try.

She smiles again. "Nope. Just have a seat. They'll call you back in a sec."

"C'mon." Elana tugs on my arm and we find two chairs near the clinic door.

"I don't want your brother paying for this," I tell her as soon as we're seated.

"He won't even know he's paying. This is my doctor. Don't worry so much." She pats my arm and pulls out her phone again.

The door to the clinic opens. "Megan Reed?"

I glance up at the other patients in the room who have been waiting and heat rushes to my cheeks as I get to my feet. There's no need to rush me in; it's not an emergency.

"I'll wait here. Don't worry, he's a good guy. Just tell him what you need." Elana pushes my hip when I'm still standing there with guilt pouring through me. I don't need special treatment, and these women have been waiting.

"It'll just be a few minutes. Go on." Elana pushes me again and I finally move.

The clinic feels more like someone's home than a doctor's office. Instead of the white storage cabinets I've seen in medical offices, there are soft chestnut-stained wood cabinets like you'd see in someone's home. Even the exam room is more like a bedroom. The bed is the same as I'm used to in a gynecologist office, but instead of the crisp white paper drawn across it, there's a fitted sheet.

"Dr. Simons will be in shortly; he's just finishing next door." The nurse points to the magenta robe folded neatly at the end of the exam table. "If you'd like him to do a full exam, go ahead and put on the robe, it ties in front."

"Oh, do I need that in order to get birth control?"

"Not necessarily. Have you had an exam in the last three years?"

I nod. "In February." It's a horrible birthday present to myself, but it's the easiest way to keep from forgetting.

"Then you can probably skip it. Can I get you anything while you wait? Water? Coffee?"

Water or coffee? At the doctor's office?

I slowly shake my head.

"No. Thanks, though."

She smiles and steps out, closing the door behind her.

I'm barely seated in the chair beside the desk before there's a knock on the door and it swings open. The doctor, a middle-aged man with thick black-rimmed glasses, saunters in, grinning.

"Megan Reed. It's nice to meet you." He holds out his hand and I'm back to my feet, shaking it. "Sit. Sit." He waves me back into the chair, then takes a seat at the desk, swinging the computer screen in front of him, and starts typing away.

"Have you ever been on birth control before?" he asks as he continues to type. "I don't see anything here in your history."

My history? How can he have my medical records already? I haven't told anyone how to get them.

"Once when I was right out high school, but I got a lot of cramping, so I stopped."

"Hmm." He nods and goes back to clicking on the screen. "Do you remember what it was?"

"No. Sorry."

"Not a problem." He leans past the screen to smile at me, then goes back to his computer.

"I have a question, though. I've had unprotected sex recently. If I somehow got pregnant, will this medication hurt the baby?" I've done my best to keep from thinking about what might happen if what Alexander and I did this morning resulted in a baby, but now that I'm sitting in this office, the reality can't be ignored.

"At this early of a stage, the hormones in the pill won't do any harm, but if you're concerned, you can wait until after your next period to start the medication," he explains. "If you do that, you'll want to be sure to use other protection in the meantime."

Right. Fat chance of that happening.

Alexander seems hell-bent on staking a claim on me in every way he can. The possessiveness in his eyes when he mentioned putting a baby in my belly gave me the impression I wouldn't be walking away from him if it happened.

This is ridiculous. I shouldn't be sitting here getting birth control. I should be asking this doctor to help me get away from Alexander. Or maybe I can just exit through the back of the office and head down to the street.

Elana is sweet, and Alexander will be pissed at her, but I can't worry about that. I need to concern myself with getting out of this enormous mess I've found myself in.

With a new plan in mind, I resolve to get it done.

"Okay. Can you give me a paper script? I'm not sure which pharmacy I'm going to use."

"Oh, no need. The medication will be delivered to the house." He smiles like he's just done me some huge favor.

"You don't need—" My sentence gets cut off when the door to the exam room bursts open and Alexander stands in the doorway.

My heart skids to a stop. Every bit of life drains from my body as I take in his rage-filled eyes and the intensity of his clenched jaw.

"Alexander." I barely get his name out of my mouth without throwing up.

His eyes sweep over me but land on the doctor.

"Mr. Volkov." Dr. Simons gets up from the desk and faces off with Alexander. I knew he was large, but holy hell. Standing in front of the doctor, he looks like the friggin' hulk.

"Is she sick?" he demands, still not looking at me.

The door is open behind him, but I have very little confidence I'd be able to get past him and through it.

"No. Not at all. I haven't done an exam but there's no concerns as of yet." He swallows as he slips his hands into the front pockets of his light-gray lab coat.

"No exam?" Alexander's jaw softens a bit.

"No. There isn't a need, unless—"

"No. There's no need."

"Alexander." I start to stand, but he finally swings his gaze toward me and it has me planting my ass right back in the chair. I'm not ready to face him just yet. His eyes are still on fire.

"Would you still like me to have the medication sent to the house?" Dr. Simons asks him, completely ignoring me now that the great and powerful Alexander Volkov is in the room.

"There's no need." Alexander takes a small step to the side. "She's finished here."

"No." I firm my jaw. "I'm not. The doctor is giving me a prescription and I'd prefer you wait outside."

Or not at all. Getting out of this office without him seeing me is going to be impossible now. He'll probably have his men waiting downstairs.

"The doctor has other patients." Alexander slowly raises an eyebrow.

"Yeah. I'm one of them." I jump to my feet, running purely on adrenaline. How dare he barge into my exam! "You should just go. This could take a while. I should have a full exam, and you don't need to be here for that."

"A full exam?" His voice softens. "You think I'm going to let you get naked and lie on this fucking table for him?" He takes a small step in my direction.

"He's a doctor!" I swing my arm in Dr. Simons' direction. The poor man looks ready to vomit.

"Get your purse. We're leaving."

"No. I'm not." I stand my ground. My legs shake a little, and my stomach is definitely rolling with nerves, but I'm still standing.

"Dr. Simons." He keeps his dark eyes locked on me while he speaks to the doctor. "You're done here."

"Yes. I see that. If there's anything you need, just call the office." Dr. Simons slips past Alexander, not sparing me a glance as he heads out, softly closing the door behind him.

"You can't just do that. I have every right." I jab my finger at him. "Every right to get birth control!"

His eyes narrow slightly.

"You've caused enough trouble for one day. Let's go." He reaches for my arm, but I swing to the side, just barely avoiding his grasp.

"No. I'm done, Alexander. I'm done!" To prove my point, I stomp my foot. This man has turned me into a crazy person, a crazy, immature brat. I haven't stomped my foot since I was a kid.

His hands rest on the buckle of his belt.

"I'm not going to argue with you, Megan. You either leave willingly with me right now, or you leave dangling over my shoulder as I carry you out. Either way, you and I are going home."

"I am home! Well, close to it anyway. Your home isn't my home!"

Another narrowing of his eyes.

"I thought I made it clear that you belong to me now."

"Belong to you?" The question comes out as a whisper. "Why?"

"Dexter Thompson was murdered." He takes a small step toward me. "Killed. And you are the only person who knows Marco DeAngelo was looking for dirt on him. Which means you are a loose end for Marco, not to mention the fucking money you owe him."

I blink back frustrating tears. This isn't happening.

"I don't know anything about anything."

"Marco isn't going to see it that way," he says. "I'm going to fix it."

I swallow, knowing I don't want to know but I have to ask.

"How? How can you fix this?"

"By making you my wife."

TWENTY

ALEXANDER

"I am not marrying you." Megan's voice barely rises over the sound of the heat blowing from the vents of my Bentley.

"I heard you the first dozen times you've said it." I turn the heat down to a lower setting now that the car's properly warmed. In her haste to get to the doctor with my sister, she hadn't brought a jacket, and the fall air is crisp.

"I'm serious. I need to be sure you understand. I will not marry you." She turns in her seat to look at me.

"I understand you think that. Yes." I turn down the alley leading to Pulse.

Megan's determination to get her ass punished continues to amaze me. Getting my sister to take her out of the house and then to a doctor that would give her birth control? My jaw clenches thinking about it.

"I'm serious, Alexander. It's not happening."

Ignoring her for the moment, I pull into the underground garage. I park next to Ivan's Aston Martin and turn off the ignition, grabbing her arm before she can think to get out of the car.

"Are we at Obsidian?" she asks, ducking her head and looking around the garage. It's only large enough for half a dozen cars. It's not meant for general parking.

"I have a meeting that I couldn't push in order to take you home, so you'll stay in my office." I put a finger up. "In my office and nowhere else, do you understand me?"

She rolls her eyes. "You know, if you'd just let me go, you wouldn't have to worry about where I was or what I was doing all the time."

While it's a fair point, it's irrelevant. She's not going anywhere.

Marco DeAngelo won't just kill her if he gets his hands on her now. He'll hurt her, torture her, do all sorts of horrible things to her before he considers killing her.

"I don't have to worry now either. Because you're going to stay in my office like a good girl."

Another eye roll. She's only been with Elana for half a day and already the attitude is wearing off on her. And Megan had plenty of her own to start with.

"Are you going to let me go home like a good boy?" She twists her lips into a sarcastic grin, like she's just won some contest.

Wrapping my hand around her throat, I drag her toward me, putting just enough pressure for her to feel the power I have over her breathing. Her eyes widen. The black of her pupils wash away those pretty irises of hers just as my mouth crushes hers.

Fuck, she's an addiction. There's fear here, just the tiniest bit, but enough for me to want to feast on her. But it's more than that. It's the sweetness of her, the beautiful way her body softens beneath my strength.

When I break the kiss, her eyes flitter open and find mine. I squeeze her throat, just a fraction.

"Never for a second think I'm anything more than what I am." It's a warning.

"You're an asshole." She blinks and a tear slips down her cheek. I release her throat and wipe the tear away with my thumb, bringing it to my lips and licking the salty moisture.

"Worse." I pop open my door. "I'm the asshole who's going to marry you."

I climb out of the car and round the back to her side before she can get the door open.

"There has to be another way." She accepts my hand when I offer it to help her out, then quickly drops it. "I'll figure out something else."

I cup her elbow and lead her to the entrance of Obsidian. There's no point to this discussion. She's not going anywhere. She's not going to figure out anything. She's going to be my wife, and the sooner she accepts it, the better.

"Don't the police ever want to come in here and see what's going on?" she asks as we walk down the corridor to my office. Her fingers drag along the stone wall.

"No."

"What happens down there exactly?" She stops at the winding staircase that would bring her down to the heart of the club. I tug her along.

"Nothing you need to know about because you're going to stay in my office. Right?" I squeeze her elbow.

A sigh is her only reply.

"Marco's expecting me to pay the money he says Mira owes. As far as he knows, I don't even know about this Dexter guy being dead. And you said yourself it was heart attack."

"I said it's being covered up as a heart attack."

"Well, either way. How would I know if it's a cover-up? I

wouldn't. So, I really only have the one problem of the money." The faint scent of my soap hits me as she sweeps past me and into my office.

I like having my scent on her. I was going to have her give the housekeeper a list of things she wanted from the store, shampoos, lotions, and such, but I might have to rethink that idea.

"And do you have the money he says you owe him?" I shut the door behind me and lean against it as she paces around the room, inspecting her surroundings.

"No." She pauses at the painting hanging on the wall of my family home back in Russia. My mother had it commissioned before my father proved himself to be the bastard that he was.

"Then I don't see how your situation has improved." I move across the room to stand beside her and point to the painting she's admiring. "My father was raised there."

"And you? Were you raised here?" she questions.

"Mostly. My father brought us here when I was a baby, but each summer he'd send my brothers and me back home to Russia to stay with our grandparents. I still return there during the summer to visit our family home."

"That's probably why your accent isn't as thick as Gregor's. It was hard to understand him sometimes, but I don't even hear it with you most of the time." Megan reminding me of her little adventure with my sister tenses my muscles. If DeAngelo had happened to see her while they were out, she could have been taken. Elana could have been hurt.

"Gregor only came to this country last year," I say.

"Maybe I could work for you. Well, not for you, but the club? You know, until Mira pops back up." She spins around so fast she knocks right into my chest. I grab hold of her arms and steady her so she doesn't bounce onto the floor.

163

"Work for the club?" It's not going to happen, but I have a few minutes before my meeting, and this might be amusing.

"Yeah. I can waitress, or I can work on the housekeeping staff, or I can—" She stops talking when I start shaking my head.

"No. To all of that."

"Well, what about downstairs? You must have different staff down there, and I bet I could make more money down there than up here anyway."

Red blurs the edges of my vision at the idea of her being down there with all the men who enjoy their time there.

"No." I drop the word hard so there's no mistaking my meaning.

"Then I can get a loan. My credit score is better than it was before; I'm sure I can get a personal loan. Then I— Stop shaking your head at me. I'm trying to find a solution!"

"I've already told you the solution." I move to my desk.

"Yes, but your solution is insane."

Pulling open the bottom drawer, I glance up at her. "My solution keeps you alive."

"There's no reason for him to hurt me if I pay him back. You're just trying to scare me into doing what you want. And why the hell would you want to marry me anyway?" She crosses her arms over her chest and sticks out a hip.

"You have a point. You're stubborn beyond reason, disobedient, and reckless with your safety." I tick off each item with a finger as her cheeks redden.

"You see, you don't want to marry me," she insists, her hands fisted at her sides. "Then why not just let me go!"

I go back to looking through my drawer until I find what I need and pull it out, shoving the drawer closed.

"Because."

Her eyes widen with my answer, and it's almost too fucking sexy to ignore. She might actually explode one of these times.

"Because?" Her left eye twitches a little at the corner.

"Yes." I give a hard nod and bring the coil of rope into her line of sight. "Now. Are you going to promise me that you'll stay here in my office while I'm gone?"

Her eyes narrow on the rope.

"Are you threatening to tie me up?" She points at the hemp rope coiled in my hands. Her anger bubbles up again. "Who keeps rope in their desk drawer!?"

"Considering the afternoon you had, do you blame me?" I put the rope on the table beside an armchair. "Promise you'll stay in here, and I won't have to use it."

"You'd believe me if I promised?" She's right. So far, she hasn't given me any reason to trust her.

"I could just tie you up, but I'm giving you a chance here." If she only understood what a rare thing this is. Then maybe she'd stop looking as though I've grown a second head.

The door to my office swings open and Ivan waltzes in, pausing when he sees the scene before him.

"I'm interrupting." He doesn't leave. Of course he doesn't. He probably finds this entire thing fucking hilarious.

One day he'll have a woman who drives him insane the way this one does me. And when he does, he'll understand why letting her go just isn't a fucking option.

She swings her gaze over to him and immediately softens, gifting him with a sweet smile.

"Hey, Ivan."

"Megan." He nods. "How's the ankle?"

"It's better," she answers. The wheels are turning in that beautiful mind of hers.

"He's not going to assist you." I check my watch. Our

meeting will be here soon, and I still haven't gotten her reassurance that she'll stay put.

"I wasn't going to ask him," she snaps. "Where's Elana? Is she here too? Maybe she can wait with me."

"My other brother, Kaz, took her home. You two aren't exactly the best influences on each other," I explain. In the car, she'd assumed Elana was with Gregor and I didn't correct her.

"So, you're going to keep the only sane person I currently know away from me?"

I can practically hear Ivan's arrogant grin behind me.

"If that's what you want to believe." I lift a shoulder. "We have a meeting to get to. Stay here, unless you'd like me to use that." I point to the rope.

She folds her arms across her chest and plops down into the armchair, crossing her legs.

"I'll sit here like a good little prisoner."

"Fiancée," I point out. "You're not my prisoner anymore; you're my fiancée."

She blusters, then looks away. "Just go to your meeting. When you come to your senses, let me know."

Not willing to miss my chance, I lean over her, cupping her chin and forcing her pretty blue eyes on me.

"Be a good girl and I'll make you scream with pleasure." I brush my lips across hers, then bring them to her ear. "But be a naughty girl and I'll make you cry with regret."

I press another kiss her to cheek and leave her sitting on the chair. Ivan arches an eyebrow when I pass him, but he follows without comment, shutting the door behind us.

"You think she'll stay put?" he asks as we reach the lounge at the far end of the corridor.

"Not a chance."

Twenty-One

MEGAN

As soon as I open the office door, a man steps in front of me, his arms folded over his chest.

"I just need the restroom." I assure the enormous man who I'm sure doubles as a bouncer for the club.

"It's down the hall, on the right." He steps back and nods in the direction I should take.

"Thanks. Back in a minute." I wiggle my fingers at him as I head off down the hall. When I glance back over my shoulder, I find him only a few paces behind me. "You don't need to come with me."

He shrugs his massive shoulders. "Alexander said to be sure you stayed in his office."

"I'll be right back. I don't think your boss would be happy with you coming into the bathroom with me."

He grins. "I'll stay outside."

Oh, for fuck's sake.

At least I'm being allowed out of the room to go to the bathroom without having a metal bucket kicked at me.

After I finish in the bathroom, my prison guard escorts me back toward the office. We're almost there when his phone goes off and he stops to answer.

"Yeah?" He gestures for me to go into the office, but no deal. I'll wait. The less I'm locked up in that room, the better.

His eyes darken, but it's not at me. It's because of whatever he's being told on the phone. I can't understand the conversation because he switches to Russian. But whatever it is, he's pissed about it.

"You need to go back into the office and stay there." He points to my new cell. Just because there's no bars on it and the door isn't locked, doesn't make it any less than a cage.

"What's wrong? Is Alexander all right?" Maybe his meeting didn't go well. The men he was supposed to be sitting down with are dangerous. Not more so than him, I doubt there's another man alive who could make Alexander nervous. But things don't always go as planned.

"He's fine," the brute assures me. "But another one of our men has been hurt. I need to see to him. You need to stay in the office." He stalks past me and shoves the door open. "Just stay inside."

I don't miss the little plea in his voice.

"Maybe I can help."

"You can't. Just stay here." He jerks his head toward the opening.

If one of their men is really hurt, every second he wastes on me is a second that man might need. Without any more argument from me, I enter the office, and the door is slammed behind me.

Pacing through the office, frustration simmers as I inspect the same four walls I've already scrutinized too many times. I drop into Alexander's chair and pull out a piece of paper. With no computer, television, or even a damn radio, I'm left to create my own distraction.

Being an only child, there were plenty of times I needed to entertain myself. I grab a pen from the cup on the desk and get to work on sketching a familiar design I used to doodle in my notebooks. Nothing distinguishable, just jagged lines that connect at random intervals.

If I had colored pencils I could make a sort of stained glass look, but the black pens will have to do.

At the bottom of the page, I sign my name, then pause when I get to my last name.

I briefly hesitate, then scribble Volkov. Just to see what it looks like.

Megan Volkov.

Not horrible.

It's at this point the pen decides to leak all over my hand. Well, crap. I drop the pen onto the paper. I need to wash this off before I get it on my clothes or on any of the furniture.

My guard still isn't back, and the hallway is empty, so I take myself down to the bathroom and wash off as much of the ink as I can.

The corridor is quiet when I step back out. I look down toward the office, then to the other side toward the stairwell we passed when we first arrived.

A loud crash captures my attention, and I pause, considering my options. Alexander made himself clear on what he would do if he caught me outside his office.

"Shit. Shit. Shit!" A female's panicked voice wafts up the stairwell.

Decision made. If she's being hurt, I'm not sure how much help I can be, but I'm sure as hell not going to stand by as one of these arrogant pricks tries to hurt her.

When I get to the bottom of the stairwell, I find

myself in a small foyer with an open door leading into a large room. A woman kneels on the floor, examining her palm.

"Are you all right?" I hurry into the lounge, taking in the dark-red and black leather chairs with a hasty glance. She's kneeling beside one of the tables.

Her cheeks blanch when she finds me standing over her.

"Who are you?" she questions immediately.

"I'm Megan. I heard the crash." I gesture to the tray of broken glass beer steins surrounding her on the black marble flooring.

She looks down at it.

"My toe caught on one of the chairs and sent me flying." She grimaces and went back to checking out her palm where she is bleeding.

"You cut yourself." I squat down beside her.

"It's fine." Blood drips down her hand and rolls off her wrist onto the floor.

"It doesn't look fine." I look around for a napkin but find nothing. "Where's the kitchen or a bathroom? You need something to wrap around your hand."

"What the fuck happened?" A familiar booming voice shakes the glass on the tray from behind me.

I sigh, then slowly turn around, still squatting.

"The steins broke, and she cut her hand," I try to explain, but he's glaring down at me from the entrance as though I've committed the worst of all sins.

I suppose to him I have. I didn't obey his little command to stay in the office.

"How bad is it?" Ivan pushes past Alexander to get to us.

"They're all broke." The woman frowns and looks down at all the shattered glass.

"Not the steins. Your hand." Ivan's voice tenses as he squats down, grabbing her wrist to inspect the injury himself. "It's deep."

"It will be fine. I need to wash it, though." She starts to stand, and he still doesn't let go of her hand.

"Put it up over your head to slow the bleeding." Ivan raises her arm up into the air. "Let's go."

"I can handle it," she argues, but he just keeps walking with her, holding her wrist up.

"Don't touch that," Alexander snaps when I reach for the broken shards, thinking to finish cleaning up the mess.

I pull my hand back and get to my feet.

"I was just helping."

"You're supposed to be in my office." He shakes his head. "Just once. Just one fucking time would you listen?"

"I went to the bathroom, and I heard the glasses crash. I only came down because I heard her. She's hurt." I jerk my hand in the direction Ivan had taken her.

Now that I'm standing and not distracted by the injured woman, I take in my surroundings.

"Oh my God." It's like I've stepped into another world.

Every inch of the club drips with elegance. Crystal chandeliers hang from the black marble ceiling. Walls trimmed in gold. It should be too much, but it's the perfect amount of sex appeal and elegance.

"That guy, the first night when I was in that room, he said something about an auction." I step over the broken glass; the implications sink like lead in my stomach. Everything makes an awful kind of sense now.

"Is that... were you auctioning off women?" I'm not sure what I expected to find down here, but not this.

"I should have tied you to my desk." The darkness of his expression sends a chill down my spine. He doesn't even have the moral compass to look guilty.

"You put women in these cages? And the men... what...? They drink and play cards and when they feel the need to get their dick wet, they take one out to play with?" I wrap my hands around the thick black metal bars of one of the cages.

"The women put themselves in the cages."

What? Why? They wouldn't possibly do that unless they had to, right? "And that makes it better?"

"Megan. A lot of things happen down here. Some of it you won't like; some of it you'll be indifferent to, and none of it is any of your business." He steps around the glass and heads straight for me.

"Where are the women now? Do you have them locked up in one of your tower rooms?" I look toward the hallway where Ivan took the girl. "Is that girl one of them?"

He stops and heaves a breath.

"I don't sell women." Each word is said with finality. Like it's important that I believe him.

He stands in front of me, so close that my back is pressed against the wall of the cage.

"You just rent them out." It's an accusation.

I curl my trembling hands into fists. He warned me about believing him to be anything more than the monster he is, but I'd almost done it anyway.

"This club is one of the most sought-after memberships in the country. Not just this city but the country." His voice dips, as though I've insulted him by degrading what he does here. "Everyone who comes here does so willingly. They pay to come here."

"You're telling me the women pay *you?*" He must think I'm a complete moron.

He stares at me a long moment, pushing his lips together while he considers telling me anything more than he already has.

"Yes. It's very much like a beauty salon. The women rent space to do whatever they want to do to make money. I don't police them. I have security here to keep them safe. That's what they pay for."

"Are you going to put me here?" It would be a good way to punish me. Sell me to the highest bidder, then he gets rid of me and any problems that come along with me. Plus, he gets the cash.

His eyes roll upward.

"My wife will never set foot down here again." He grabs my chin. His fingers pinch my cheeks into my teeth. "My wife shouldn't be down here now."

"I'm not your wife." Why do I have to keep reminding him?

"Not yet," he grounds out. "But I'm going to change that real fucking soon."

"What else happens down here?" I can't argue about a marriage that's not going to happen. Not yet.

"Business happens. Deals are made. Political alliances are kept and broken. Everything that needs to be done in the dark, is done in this room." He steps to the left and turns my face toward the doors lined up against the far wall.

"In those rooms, men and women have fantasies fulfilled. They fuck and get fucked. No one is forced." It seems to be important that I understand the last part.

I swallow hard when he drags my attention back to his face.

"That night you found me in that office, you thought I was here because of this club?"

His eyes wander over my face. "Whoever told you about that office knows about this club."

"And they could be looking for me too?"

He arches a brow. "She finally gets it. You've put powerful

men in danger of being caught, Megan. They don't like loose ends." He whispers the last part.

I stare at the doors to the fantasy rooms, imagining each one closing, the sound one of finality. I'm a loose end. I'm the unpredictable, something he can't control. Closing my eyes briefly, a sense of fatality washes over me.

"Okay. I get it. I understand." I try to pull away from his grip, but he's not done.

"Do you?"

Marco DeAngelo is one problem, but a secret danger is another. Without knowing who I should be hiding from, how can I hide?

"I do, Alexander. Really. I get it." I wrap my hand around his wrist, and he slowly lets up on his grip.

"Good." He lets my chin go, but captures my hand, lacing his fingers through mine and tugging.

"Where are we going?" I ask as he half drags me across the room, avoiding the tables as we weave in and out of them.

"You wanted to see what this place is, so I'm going to show you." He heads for one of the closed doors.

"Wait. I'm sorry. You don't need to do that." I fight his grip but there's no point. Haven't I learned yet? If he wants me somewhere, that's where I'm going.

He stops at the door, looking down at me with fire burning bright in his dark eyes. His nostrils flare a little with each deep breath he takes.

"What did I say before I left you in the office?"

I blink, trying to remember which threat he gave me today.

"You said if I was..." I swallow hard. "If I was a good girl, you'd make me scream with pleasure."

"And were you a good girl?" His hand rests on the golden door handle.

"I tried." It's barely a whisper. I can barely find my voice when his expression screams danger is ahead.

The left side of his mouth kicks up and he pushes the door handle down, opening the door to the room.

"Not good enough."

I tear my gaze away from him and glance at the room. My heart stops. I can't go in there.

I can't.

Twenty-Two

MEGAN

Alexander's long fingers squeeze around mine, a signal that he's not going to back down.

"Come. You wanted to see, let me show you." His words wrap around me like the finest silk.

But then again, the devil always was a smooth talker.

"I get it. It's a torture room." I eye the bench in the middle of the room. Black leather covers the four pads that are dropped lower than the main portion of the bench.

"No, Megan." He pulls me inside and shuts the door behind us. The soft click echoes in my ears. "Pleasure is found here."

He walks around the room, past the bench to a wooden post in the corner. A thick black ring is mounted near the top and there's a small platform at the bottom.

"Come here." He crooks a finger at me, and I retreat a step.

"I'd rather not."

"I can put you here or you can come here." His eyes bore into me, almost as though he's willing me to go to him on my own. This man can break me easily. He's already proven I'm no physical match to him.

If he wants to tie me up and beat me, he'll do it. And no one in this place will intervene.

But I'm not afraid of that, of his strength. I know I should be. And I'm sure a few sessions with a therapist are going to be in order when this whole ordeal is over, but there's more than darkness in his stare.

Desire lingers there.

Each step I take in his direction seems to please him more and more. His sinister grin twists into one of satisfaction.

"Step here." He points to the platform. "Back to the post."

"Why?"

His arrogant grin returns.

"Because."

"You're not going to spank me again?" Did I actually just sound disappointed about that? I've really lost it.

"I haven't decided what part of you to punish. But I know which parts I want to see, to touch." He leans down to my ear. "To taste."

Heat rolls through my veins and I step backward, the post hitting my back as I do.

He runs the back of his knuckles across my jawline.

"Good girl. Now remove your clothes." He glances down at the light-blue sweater I'm wearing with a pair of jeans. "All of them."

He turns his back on me, as though he just expects me to obey him. The arrogance of this man is enough to drive me crazy, and yet I find myself grabbing the hem of the sweater.

When I've pulled the sweater up over my head, I find him standing in front of me with a pair of leather cuffs connected by a long chain. My mouth dries and I hold the sweater over my chest, as though it's some sort of shield.

"What are you going to do with those?" I ask stupidly. He must realize I'm aware of how silly my question is, because all he does is arch an eyebrow at me.

"You're still dressed." He gestures toward me with his chin. Looking past him, I see a small drawer in the side of the padded bench. It's still open enough for me to see other chains and cuffs.

I shove out of my jeans and toss them onto the bench with my sweater, leaving me only in my blue cotton panties and my cream-colored bra.

Matching panty sets have never been my thing. Comfort has always overridden any sort of fashion rules. But now that I'm standing in this room with Alexander, I wish I'd taken some of the advice given in the magazines.

Alexander steps up to me, his eyes warming my skin as he looks down at me. Moving the cuffs to one hand, he brings his free hand to my shoulder, to the strap of my bra. Sliding his fingertip beneath the strap, he pulls it down over my shoulder until the cup of the bra frees my breast. Then he does the same with the other strap.

My nipples peak beneath the scrutiny of his gaze. He wraps his arm around to the back, finding the clasp of my bra. With expertise, he works the clasp open and the bra falls down the length of my arms. I catch it before it drops to the floor.

"Give me your hands," he says, stepping back enough to allow room between us.

My panties are still on, but who am I to argue?

I toss the bra onto the pile of discarded clothing and hold up my hands. He tightens the cuffs, their leather pulling softly against my wrists with the movement, and brings them through the ring over my head.

The wood is cool against my back as I lean against it.

Alexander takes a step back, raking his gaze over me. I've

never been insecure about my body. No more than anyone else, I suppose, but standing here on display like this with his eyes taking stock of me, I can't help but want to curl into myself.

He takes his time shucking out of his suit jacket and laying it across the bench. Then he undoes the cuffs of his pale-gray shirt and folds the sleeves up to his elbows. Each fold is perfect before he moves on to the next one.

"Tell me, Megan. What should I do with you?" He runs the tip of his nose along my cheek, up to my ear. "Such a naughty girl today."

My insides melt when his tongue flicks my earlobe.

"Such a bad, bad girl." He grabs hold of my hips and pushes me back against the post. "Did you really think my men wouldn't keep me informed of where you are?"

He brings his mouth to the soft flesh where my shoulder meets my neck and bites down. I wince at the sharp bite, but it's short-lived. He licks away the mark.

"Did you think you'd be allowed to do anything that would prevent my baby from taking root in your belly?" He splays his hand across my stomach and presses.

"I... You're being unreasonable." It would be easier to be more forceful if he wasn't touching me. He moves his hand from my hip to my ass, squeezing my cheek until I rise up on my toes.

"And then you leave my office when you were told to stay put. Instead. I find you down here in my club." He kisses my collarbone, then flicks a tongue over my nipple as he lowers himself to his knees in front of me.

"I... she was hurt." My words barely register they come out so weak and soft.

Alexander presses his face between my thighs, inhaling deeply.

"Such sweetness." He slips one finger beneath the thin

fabric covering my pussy and pulls it to the side. As he looks up at me, our eyes lock just before his tongue brushes across my clit.

My legs weaken, but the cuffs won't let me buckle. I press myself back against the post for support.

"This pussy." He licks his lips, then hooks his arm beneath one of my legs, pulling it up and resting it on his broad shoulder.

"Alexan—p" I can't get the rest of his name out as his tongue swirls around my clit. I roll my head back against the post, grateful for the support it gives me.

He angles his head so he can run his tongue farther through my folds, teasing the entrance of my pussy. The metal chain linking the cuffs clinks against the iron loop they're secured through as I squirm beneath his tongue.

Soft lashings across my clit drive me closer and closer to an edge I would gladly nosedive over.

"Such a naughty girl," he mutters against my pussy, flattening his tongue against my clit and rubbing it in circles.

My eyes roll back as my muscles tighten, readying for the explosion that's sure to happen.

I moan, arching my back to urge my hips toward him. I need more, just a little more.

He sucks my clit between his teeth, and I'm going to die. My heart can't hammer this hard against my ribs and let me live.

"Fuck. Fuck." I look down the length of me at this man kneeling in front of me. His dark eyes turn up at me and I'm lost to him, to the danger inside him.

"Ask, Megan. Beg for permission," he orders, slipping two fingers just inside my pussy. "Beg me."

What if he denies me again? He left me hungry and needy for a full night. If he does it again, what will I do? Will I be the good girl he seems to want, or do I continue fighting him and taking what I want?

"Just ask, baby." He runs his tongue just over the top of my clit. Nowhere enough to give me what I want, but enough for him to make me give him what he needs.

"I need to come, Alexander. Please?" My wrists strain against the cuffs as I lean forward.

His lips spread wide as he leans into my pussy again.

"Ask again," he says, swiping his tongue over me slowly.

Frustration curls my toes.

"Can I... oh fuck!" Before I can get the question out, he thrusts two fingers inside, curling them as he flicks his tongue over my clit. It's too much to ignore.

The dam breaks. Waves of pleasure drown me and I'm lost to my orgasm. He never leaves me, his tongue lightly driving me through the waves, navigating me through the intense storm of pleasure until it slowly ebbs.

He presses a soft kiss just above my pussy, then to my thigh before he puts my foot back onto the ground. More kisses trail their way up my body as he gets back to his feet.

The taste of my arousal is strong on his lips when his mouth captures mine. He bites my lower lip softly when he breaks the kiss, lightly pressing his cheek to mine.

"Naughty girl," he whispers.

The metallic jangle of a belt being unbuckled strikes my ears, cutting through the fog of my climax.

I blink his face into focus as he grins at me, stepping back and ripping his belt through the loops of his pants.

"Now your punishment can begin."

In my confusion of the sudden change of the moment, he flips me around on the post. My cheek presses against the wood.

It takes another moment before I realize what's he's doing.

And half a moment after that before the first lash of his belt lands across my ass.

I rise up on my toes, trying to get away from the fire. But there's nowhere I can go.

And it's worse. So much worse than the other times he's spanked me.

There's no arousal to dampen the pain of the leather kissing my skin. It's pure, white-hot pain striking me across my ass cheeks, my thighs, and back to my ass.

I yank on my binds, but I'm going nowhere. Twisting a bit to avoid the belt only manages to wrap the leather around my hip.

He curses and grabs my waist, putting me back into position while muttering something in Russian.

"Alexander!" I cry out as the belt lands again.

In the next second the belt clanks to the platform at my feet and his hands are on me, spinning me back around to face him.

He captures my face with both hands, pushing my head back and crashing his mouth over mine. The intensity is nothing like I've ever experienced.

His fingers dig farther into my hair as he deepens the kiss.

Everything inside of me melts. The pain blurs back into need. To be touched by him. To be fucked by him.

To be owned by him.

His pants are shoved away and again he lifts my leg into the crux of his arm.

"I need to be inside you," he mutters against my lips as he kisses me again, pushing the fat head of his cock against my entrance.

"Yes. Fuck me, Alexander. Please." I kiss him back, needing the touch of his mouth against mine while he impales me.

"Megan," he growls my name as though he's not sure he should trust himself.

"Please," I whisper my plea. "Please, Alexander." Being whipped without the arousal to mask the true punishment of the leather has made my ass more tender. But the pain drives my need to have him make it all better.

"Fuck," he groans as he slides his cock into my pussy. It's slow, the stretch and burn, and I relish it.

He pins me to the post, and I throw my head back.

"I'm not a gentle man, baby," he warns me, lining up our eyes.

"I know, Alexander. I don't want gentle," I say. "Not from you."

He pulls back just enough for the head of his dick to rest inside my pussy before he drives forward.

I cry out as he pummels into me. He's so deep it steals my breath away, but he's not one for patience. Pulling back, he drives forward again.

And again.

And again, until my core tightens and my skin is alive with electric heat. I wrap my hands around the chains of my cuffs, using it as leverage to push back at him as he thrusts.

"Fuck, baby, oh fuck." He bites down on my shoulder, and I cry out with the new pain.

"Oh God. I have to come. Please, Alexander. Please, can I come?" I beg him, not wanting to waste any time on games. I need him to drive me over the cliff, the only way he can.

He kisses my ear.

"Fucking come for me, baby. And make it loud." He bites my neck. Harder than his last bite and slams his cock into me so hard I'm shoved against the post.

He wraps his free hand around my waist and grabs my ass where his belt has left a heated sting.

And I come unraveled, throwing my head back against the post as I scream out with my release.

"Good girl." He licks my throat as the last of my orgasm fades. "Good fucking girl." He plows into me again and again and again until he stills.

Throwing his head back, he unleashes an animalistic roar as his cock spills his hot seed inside of me.

I sag against the cuffs, rolling my head to rest on one of my arms as I try to catch my breath.

Alexander eases my foot down as he slips out of me. He kisses my cheek.

"Give me a second to get you down, baby." He quickly gets the cuffs undone and off the post. He lifts me up into his arms and I rest against his chest as he wraps a blanket over me.

When did he get that out?

I'm too tired to care. I wrap my arms around his neck, nuzzling farther into him as he sits us down.

"You shouldn't be holding me like this," I say, losing myself in the warm spice of his cologne.

"No? Why is that?" He tucks the blanket tighter around me.

"It makes it harder to hate you." My eyelids are heavy, so I close them. I'll tell him later he can't keep me. I'll explain he has to let me go.

And he's just going to have to listen to me for once.

Twenty-Three

Megan

Rolling pleasure draws me from a deep sleep. My nightgown is pushed up to my hips and my legs are wrapped around Alexander's shoulders.

Blinking away the sleep, his gaze comes into focus as he looks up the length of my body at me.

"Good morning." He lifts up from my body just long enough to mutter the words.

"What are you... oh God." My eyes roll as his tongue flicks across my clit.

His hands slide beneath my ass, lifting my hips from the bed to feast on me as though he's been starved for a lifetime.

I moan with need as I press up into his mouth. He seals his lips over my clit and strokes it with his wet, hot tongue.

"Alexander." I fist the sheets at my sides, pushing up at him even more. "Oh, fuck."

He spreads my ass cheeks a little, sliding one hand between them and pushing a finger against my ass.

"Shhh, baby, let me in." He kisses the little spot just above my clit as he pushes his finger past the tight ring, into my ass.

Slowly, he pushes in and pulls back, while keeping me on the edge of pleasure with his tongue lashing over my clit.

I gasp at the sweet burn as he slips a second finger inside, stretching me as he pumps his fingers in and out of me.

"That's my good girl," he mutters against my sex as his tongue swirls over my clit, through my folds, then down to my needy entrance. I can't help but push up harder at his face.

"Do you want me to fill you there too?" he questions just as he thrusts his tongue inside.

"Oh, fuck. Yes," I groan.

"Soon, baby." He fucks my ass faster with his fingers, spreading them and stretching me while he feasts on me. Licking my clit, nibbling, sucking me hard into his mouth.

Rolling waves of pleasure run over my body, drawing me closer and closer to the edge. My skin heats and I'm sure my next breath might be my last. But then he flicks his tongue again, and I'm even tighter. I'm so fucking close to exploding, I can barely register anything other than his touch.

"Come, baby, give me what I want." He curls his fingers and sweeps his tongue across my clit, sending a shock wave of pleasure through my body as my orgasm rips through me.

Rolling my head to the side, I lie there, catching my breath. Slowly, he climbs up my body and settles beside me, pulling me into his arms and pressing a kiss to my forehead. The scent of my arousal covers his face.

As soon as my mind settles, I reach between our bodies, seeking out his cock, but he grabs my wrist.

"No. Later I will feel your lips wrapped around my cock, but not this morning. This day is special. It's for you." He strokes my hair away from my face.

"What does that mean?" I sit up a little. "Why is it for me?"

He's up to something. Last night when we finally came

home from the club, he sent me to bed alone, saying he had business to deal with. I have no idea when he finally came to bed; I was asleep before my head hit the pillow.

"You've never told me about your hair." He picks up a lock of the white strands. "It's not dyed, but there's no color."

"My mother had the same thing. She said it's called poliosis," I explain with a shrug. "I don't have any other discoloration on my skin, just those two patches in my hair."

He runs the back of his hand across my cheek.

"Your mother died when you were just out of high school, but I didn't find much information on your father."

I rest my head on his chest. "He disappeared when I was in second grade."

"What do you mean, disappeared?"

"He left us. He dropped me off at school, hugged me, and then left. He was supposed to pick me up that afternoon, but he never came. I sat in the playground waiting for him until finally a teacher noticed me still sitting there and called my mom."

His body tenses beneath me.

"The police weren't able to find him?"

"Mom didn't bother with the police. When we got home that night, his closet had been cleared out. After he dropped me off, he packed his stuff and left."

I haven't explained my father's disappearance to anyone in so long, a fresh wave of pain rolls through.

"At least he had the decency to let my mother get a divorce quickly."

"She saw him?"

"Just once. He said he couldn't handle a family, signed the papers, and left." I look up at him. "It's fine. We were fine without him."

His jaw tightens.

"I will never walk away from you, Megan," he says with such conviction, I can't help but want to believe him.

"Eventually, you'll have to. Marco has to give up at some point, right? And then I can go home, and you can go about your business."

He rolls over me, pressing my back to the mattress and framing my face with his hands.

"Marco won't give up until he has what he wants." He cocks a grin. "It's the only way we are similar."

"Alexander!" Insistent knocking breaks through the room. "The dresses are here!"

He sighs.

"Elana!" he barks, then rattles off something in Russian.

"Got it!" She knocks once more, then there's silence.

"What did you just tell her?" I ask.

"If I wanted you to know, I would have said it in English." He winks, then rolls off me.

"What did she mean, the dresses are here?" I push up to my elbows. "And what's special about today?" I recall his words only a little earlier before he distracted me.

Standing beside the bed in his black boxers, he hooks his hands on his hips.

"Today is our wedding day," he announces as though he knows a battle is about to erupt.

And he's right.

Flinging off the covers, I jump out of bed.

"Absolutely not." I slice my hand through the air. "I'm not marrying you. I told you that."

He nods. "I know what you said."

"Then why aren't you listening to me?" I glare in his direction as he casually walks around the bed toward me.

"I hear you fine, Megan. You are the one not listening." His eyes darken and I can tell this isn't going to be an easy match. But I will win this round.

He can't just expect me to marry him because he says so.

Although, he does that with pretty much everything else.

"There's no reason for you to throw away your life because I have some crazy asshole looking for me. You said you have one of your friends looking for Mira, right? When he finds her, we'll figure out a way to pay Marco off." It could work.

Marco was taking the money before, so why would he stop now? He's a business guy after all.

"You think marrying you would be throwing my life away?" Somehow, he's gotten more irritated.

He steps up to me. My body tenses beneath his hot glower, and I want to take a step back. To put more room between us. But there's no point. If he's taught me anything in these past weeks, it's if I run, he chases.

And he will always catch me.

"I think you're looking at a permanent solution to a temporary problem."

"Yesterday you seemed to finally understand the danger. But now you're pretending like the money is the only issue."

I swallow.

"Dexter Thompson's death."

"Murder, Megan. His murder," he emphasizes. "With my name, you are safe. No one would dare come after you. It will assure anyone who thinks you may speak out of turn, that your lips are sealed."

"Marco will give up because we got married?" It can't be that simple.

"Others that might side with Marco will step away from it. They would not dare go against me in this."

"Marrying you might give me protection, but what about

Mira? If he can't come after me anymore, he'll start going after her."

"Your loyalty to your friend is admirable, Megan. It's one of the things I like most about you. But in this case, you need to protect yourself first. Rurik will find her, and he will bring her home. But you're here now."

"Marriage doesn't work, Alexander." Mom tried to keep herself together after Dad walked out on us, but late at night, when she thought I was asleep, I heard her sobs. The man she'd called the love of her life had walked out without looking back.

"It can."

"How? By letting you do whatever you want, like your dad obviously did? Will I have to watch you have mistresses and watch them give birth to your children the way your mother did?"

His jaw tightens.

"I am not my father," he says so low, so raw, I know I've struck a live wire.

"And when you tire of me? When you finally break me and are bored with me, what then? Will you send me away?"

He snatches me, his hand firmly wrapped around the back of my neck as he drags me forward.

"I will bend you, Megan. But I will never break you. And life with you will never be boring. We'll fill the house with children. The girls will keep us both on our toes because they will be like you, and the boys will give us both gray hair too soon because they will be like me." He squeezes my neck.

But I can't believe him. I won't.

"And when you realize we're all too much for you?" I breathe out my question as tears threaten. I will not cry over a future that will not happen.

"I would never walk away from you, from our family," he vows.

"Alexander. You don't want this; you don't want me. You're only trying to protect me." I pause. "When the danger is gone, you might change your mind."

He kisses my cheek. "My mind is made up. The judge will be here this afternoon. We'll stand before my family, and we'll speak our vows."

"And what I want has no meaning? Still?"

His sigh is heavy.

"I will do whatever it takes to keep you safe. If I have to drag you downstairs and force you to say the words at gunpoint, I will do it to keep you safe." He moves his hand to my cheek. "I will protect you, even from yourself."

"I can say no. You know that's an option, right?" I point out.

"I know you can try, yes." He nods and walks to the closet.

"The judge won't marry us if I say no," I call after him when the inner light flicks on and he's stepped inside.

"You can believe that if it makes it easier for you." He walks back in wearing a pair of jeans and pulling on a black t-shirt. His dark hair is mussed once the shirt's on and he combs it back with his fingers.

"There are a dozen dresses for you to choose from. Pick whichever one you want. Elana will be up with them and she can help you." He opens the top drawer of the dresser and pulls out a pair of socks.

"There's no need for all that."

He stops at the door, the socks and a pair of shoes in one hand.

"Be dressed and ready by four o'clock. The judge will be here, and we'll have it all done and settled by five."

"All done and settled? But I haven't even agreed yet!"

"I'm not worried." He flashes an arrogant grin. "Four o'clock, Megan." He winks and leaves me to seethe all alone in his beautiful, gigantic bedroom.

Twenty-Four

Alexander

She wears black to our wedding.

Kaz laughs behind me as I watch my bride and my sister walk down the winding staircase together. Elana has a worried smile on her lips while my bride stares me down as she steps onto the landing in the foyer.

"I guess we know how the bride feels about the wedding." Kaz smacks my back, then walks over to Elana to get her out of the line of fire.

If she thinks a little wardrobe tantrum will alter the plans, she's about to be disappointed.

Megan makes her way to me with a smug smile firmly on her lips.

"Do you like it?" She runs her hands over the black beading of the bodice that gives way to a large skirt. None of her curves are noticeable in this black tent she's wearing. The neckline is basically up to her chin.

"Where did you find it?" The dresses I had brought over from Vira Wang Bridal for her to choose from did not have this monstrosity among them.

"You don't like it?" She feigns a frown and looks down at the dress. "The beads are so pretty, though." One of them pops off as she plays with it, and it rolls across the floor. "Oops."

"If this is the dress you want to get married in, who am I to say anything about it?" Another ping sounds as a bead falls to the floor at my feet.

"She still has time to change," Elana says. "Maybe we should look at the rack again."

"No." Megan keeps her eyes trained on me as she shakes her head. "I like this one."

"If this is what she wants to wear, I'll allow it." I'm gifted with the fire only her eyes can burn at my words. She couldn't have thought I would stop the wedding because of a repulsive dress. The woman beneath the mountain of fabric is anything but, and once the vows are spoken, I'll get her out of it.

"You'll allow it?" The fake excitement is a bit much, even for her. "Oh, gee, thanks, daddy."

Leaning down so only she can hear me, I say, "Keep it up, and I'll put you over daddy's knee and spank you right here. Then you can spend the rest of the day in the corner like a naughty little girl should."

Fuck. What had started out as a way to deter her from letting her attitude get any more out of hand, has turned into a raging hard-on.

I think she's going to have to spend some time in the corner when I get rid of my siblings. Just for good measure.

"What a beautiful bride," Judge Slovene pipes up from his position near the fireplace after our glaring match continues. "If you're both ready?"

"We are." I step to her side and cup her elbow, trying not to step on the puddle of fabric at her feet.

"I'm not sure. I might need more time." She tugs slightly,

but I firm my grip. If I have to chase this woman anymore, I'm going to tie her to me.

"She doesn't," I assure him, half dragging her across the living room. His eyebrows rise slightly, but one shake of my head and he settles his features. His consent to this marriage isn't needed, and I can only fight one battle at a time.

"You should know, he's threatened to shoot me if I don't marry him," she announces once we're standing in front of him.

The judge schools his features, but I can see his throat work as he swallows back his conscience.

"You can begin." I gesture to him.

He clears his throat and begins.

"Marriage is a commitment to share your life together and to grow with each other in a lifelong partnership. Today, you are committing to that union, to love, honor, and cherish one another."

Her body goes rigid as the judge speaks. She believes marriages can't work, and ours isn't exactly starting off with any sort of fairy-tale romance.

"Do you, Alexander Volkov, take Megan Reed to be your lawfully wedded wife, to live together in marriage, to honor her and to protect her with your very life if needed, in sickness and in health for as long as you both shall live?"

Her brow wrinkles when she hears the vows I altered for our wedding. The standard commitment didn't fit for us, and she needs to know I mean what I say when I speak these words.

I wait until she brings those sparkly blue eyes of hers to meet mine before answering.

"I do."

"And do you, Megan Reed, take Alexander Volkov, to be your lawfully wedded husband, to live together in marriage, to honor him, to cherish him, and to obey him, in sickness and in health for as long as you both shall live?"

Her lips pinch together.

"Obey him?" She starts to pull away again, but I bring her back, steadying her before she can trip on that god-awful dress.

"Say the words, Megan," I warn.

She blows out a heavy sigh with an added eye roll.

"Fine."

Elana giggles from somewhere behind me, matching Kaz's laughter over the whole thing. One day he'll find a woman who turns him inside out like this one does me, and then we'll see who's laughing.

"I think that's as good as you're getting, Judge," Ivan says when the judge seems to be waiting for the right response from Megan. "Let's wrap it up."

The judge takes another peek at Megan's glower and nods.

"Right. By the power vested in me, I now pronounce you husband and wife. You may uh... well... kiss the bride."

He hasn't even gotten the last word out before I wrap my hand around her neck and pull her to me. At first, her hands push against my chest, but it only takes a little nibble to her lip to get her to soften against me.

When I break the kiss, she stares up at me for a moment, and I wish I could hear her thoughts. They seem to be all jumbled together. The thing about Megan is having a clear line works best. When there's too much at one time, she doubts herself. And then she gets herself into trouble.

She lets out a little sigh.

I release her and she turns to the judge.

"So, do I go directly to you for a divorce, or should I get an attorney?" she asks Judge Slovene. Panicked eyes meet mine when he looks over her shoulder at me.

I can't help the little smile pulling on my lips. I fold my arms over my chest as I await his answer.

He clears his throat.

"Well, I don't usually handle that sort of thing..." he trails off with a plea in his gaze as he sweeps the room.

"She's kidding," Elana assures him, rushing forward and grasping Megan by the arm.

"Not really." Megan lifts a shoulder.

"I'll walk you out." Ivan steps in and gives the judge an exit strategy. He shoots me a glare as he follows the judge from the living room to the foyer.

When Megan finally turns to me, her features have softened slightly. "I should go change."

"No. Absolutely not." I grab her hand, bringing it up to my mouth, and kiss her knuckles. "I've had Mrs. Wells make a special meal for us. It's waiting in the dining room."

She frowns.

"It will only take a few minutes." She glances over at Elana, looking for help I assume, but it's not going to come from that corner of the room.

"People are waiting for us." I firmly plant her arm through mine and pull her along.

"What does that mean?" She doubles her efforts to stop, but I'm stronger and more than willing to carry her if need be. She wanted to play games, why stop now?

When we get to the double doors of the dining room, Elana comes to stand behind my wife.

"I told you not to wear that ugly thing," she whispers.

Megan twists her neck to look at Elana, then back at me.

"What's going on?"

Megan

"*Pozdravlyaem!*" The dining room is filled with the Volkov men and a handful of women.

I freeze at the door.

"You should have listened to me," Elana whispers again.

"You could have told me about this," I mutter back at her.

"What's wrong, wife?" Alexander squeezes my hand.

"You're trying to humiliate me," I accuse, but there isn't much fire behind the words. Hadn't I just done the same thing by wearing this atrocity to the ceremony?

There's a crush of people making their way toward us, many speaking to Alexander in Russian. I'm barely acknowledged other than a quick glance before they give their congratulations to him.

"Congratulations on your wedding." A man hands Alexander an envelope.

Alexander takes the gift and hands it off to Kaz who holds several other envelopes. Most of the men make a quick greeting before heading away from us, but this man switches to Russian and draws Alexander into a conversation.

"Who was that?" I ask when they finally stop talking and the man rejoins a smaller group in the far corner of the room.

"His name is Oleg, one of my men." Alexander gestures toward a waitstaff carrying a tray of champagne glasses.

"He didn't even look at me. None of them did," I comment when Alexander hands me a glass of champagne during a short interlude of well-wishers.

"Because if their eyes linger longer than appropriate, even for a second, I'll have them cut from their heads." He speaks with such sincerity, but he has to be joking. He's not that mad, is he?

"That's a little extreme." I try to laugh off his ridiculous comment. "Even for you."

After I down the champagne, he removes the flute from my hand.

"It's my way, Megan. What's mine is mine, and I will do whatever I have to in order to keep it safe." His eyes are firm when he says this. He's told me this before, but it's different somehow this time. Like his words are heavier now that I bear his last name.

"A lingering look isn't dangerous," I nearly whisper. His possessive glare has me captivated.

"It is for them." He places my empty flute on the table. "Dinner will be served soon. Go up and change into something else. I think we've both made our points."

I look around the large dining room with the extended table with settings for twenty. These are his men and their wives, and they've come to congratulate him on his marriage. It's important, I'm sure, to make this event somewhat public so word will travel that he's married me, but these are his men. No matter how pissed he makes me, trying to embarrass him with this dress was in bad taste.

"Thanks. I'll be back in twenty." I pick up the massive amount of fabric of the skirt and make my way to the doors. Elana is at my side as soon as I'm in the hall.

"I'll help you." She smiles and takes some of the burden of the fabric as we head through the house back up to Alexander's bedroom.

Well, our bedroom now, I suppose.

"I can't believe you actually wore this thing." Elana laughs as she grapples with the antique zipper.

"If you had told me there was going to be all those other

people, I wouldn't have." I step out of the dress once it's pooled at my feet and head over to the rack of dresses he had brought over from Vera Wang.

VERA WANG!

I've never been a fashionista, but even I understand the luxury of wearing a Vera Wang wedding dress.

"I didn't know, to be honest. I knew he asked Mrs. Wells to make a special dinner, but he didn't mention all those people. It was only when he brought us to the larger dining room that I realized what was happening." Elana kicks the black dress into the corner of the room.

"He's just so... so... demanding." I grit my teeth a little with the memory of his dictates about getting married. "I mean, he didn't ask me to marry him, Elana. He demanded it. He said I had to. I wasn't lying about the threat to shoot me."

She stops sorting through the dresses to give me an exasperated look.

"He wouldn't shoot you."

"You don't know that. He's shot at me before," I tell her. "Well, it was a shot in the air because I was running away from him, but still."

She laughs. "That sounds like him. When I was about eight, our dad sent Alexander's mom to Russia for the summer. He made me come stay with him for a month. Now my father never gave me the time of day, so I have no idea why he did that, especially since he didn't even spend any time with me that month. He pawned me off on the boys."

"That had to be hard, having a father like that." Would Alexander be that way to our children? I shake the thought from my head. This isn't going to last long enough for children. Once the danger passes, he has to come to his senses.

She lifts a shoulder. "I got used to it pretty quick. He at least didn't ignore me financially. But anyway, I was so mad that I had to be here instead of home with my friends, I ran away. Or at least I tried. Alexander found me two blocks away. He didn't say anything. The big brute just walked right up to me, picked me up, and carried me home."

I laugh at the image of a twenty-four-year-old Alexander carrying his little sister down the street.

"Did he yell at you?"

"No." She laughs. "He just brought me to my room and told me to stay put."

"Well. You're his sister, of course he was protective and overbearing to you." I pick out an ivory strapless drop-waist A-line gown with a black horsehair sash. It's one of the most beautiful dresses I've ever seen with feathered tulle flower embroidery not only on the skirt but on the bodice buttons on the back.

Elana takes the dress from my hands and lays it on the bed to start unbuttoning the back bodice.

"He's like that with those he cares about, Megan. That's what I'm telling you." She slides the hanger from the dress and tosses it on the bed. "I know he forced you down there today, and it's not what you wanted, but he only goes to these extremes for people he really cares about. If he didn't give a shit about you, he wouldn't have just married you."

"Well, it's temporary."

She freezes and turns a raised eyebrow at me. "If you really believe that, you're lying to yourself. Alexander took vows down there, and he takes his vows seriously."

Before I can argue that this is all really unnecessary, my phone vibrates on the nightstand. Hoping it's Mira finally checking in, I grab it and swipe the screen to life.

Time's up. Where's the drive?

Twenty-Five

Alexander

Inside the walk-in closet, Megan stands in front of the full-length mirror when I join her in our bedroom. The guests have finally left, my siblings the last of them.

Leaning my shoulder against the doorframe, I take her in.

She's changed out of the Vera Wang dress into a black satin nightgown. Lace trims the neckline and the hem that barely kisses the edge of her ass.

When she turns to the side, inspecting herself, she catches me in the reflection and her cheeks redden.

"I was just trying it on." She flattens her hands over her stomach. "It's too nice, I can't keep it."

"It's not going back to the store, so if you don't wear it, it will just go to waste." She grew up without excess and without the luxury she deserves. That stops now. I'm going to drape this woman in diamonds, silks, and at night—leather.

She glances back at the mirror. "This is all too much, Alexander. The dress, and now the nightgowns."

"It's not enough, but we can argue about it later. I'm not in the mood for it now." Her nipples pebble beneath the satin fabric and all I can think about now is peeling the damn thing off her to get to them.

"Rurik wasn't here tonight, at least I don't remember his name when you were introducing me to people." She tucks her hair behind her ears, while her toes curl into the lush carpeting.

Is she nervous to be alone with me? After everything we've gone through up until today, it's standing in a nightgown on our wedding night that frightens her?

"No. I spoke with him this afternoon, before you came downstairs. So far, he's not been able to locate Mira, but he will," I reassure her. I have a few questions for Mira when he does.

Like how the hell she thought it was okay to leave town and let a man like Marco DeAngelo unleash himself on Megan in her stead.

"She still hasn't gotten a hold of you?" I don't need to ask the question, but she's my wife now. Too many years I watched lies fly back and forth between my parents in their marriage. I won't have it in mine.

She lets out a little sigh and turns back to the mirror, tugging on the hem. A soft pink blush touches the spot on her neck that gives her away whenever she's trying to be dishonest.

I relax my features, waiting for whatever lie she seems to be cooking up.

"I have to tell you something." She faces me, her fingers flexing at her sides. "But before I do, can you promise me that you won't get all Russian Mafia about it?"

I arch a brow. "How can I promise that when I don't know what it is you want to tell me?"

"Because I don't want to lie to you or hide things from you.

You've made a big sacrifice today, marrying me in order to keep me safe. I want to trust you. Please just promise you won't order me to be locked away with an armed guard outside my door just because you think it will make me safer."

Marrying her isn't the sacrifice she seems to believe it is. This woman was mine the moment I took the cat mask off her at Obsidian.

"I will promise to react with the appropriate amount of Russian Mafia. Does that work for you?" I slide my hands into my front pockets. The benefit of having her phone mirrored to mine is I already know what she wants to show me.

I'd hoped she would tell me on her own, but I expected her to take longer. This show of trust won't go unrewarded. Throwing her in a locked tower, while appealing in some senses, would serve more to push her away.

After another moment of thought, she heaves a sigh. "I guess I'll take it."

I move to the side as she brushes past me and into the bedroom, where she pulls her phone out of the nightstand drawer. Swiping it to life, she brings it back to me and shows me the screen.

I glance at the text message she received hours ago. When it came through on my phone, my immediate reaction was to find her and tie her to my side. But when there was no response from her to the message, I decided to give her the benefit of the doubt.

My bet was right.

"I don't know if it's from Marco or not. It didn't come through from his phone." She frowns. "Maybe he has a new one."

I take the phone from her hands and press the side button, powering it down.

"We'll deal with it tomorrow." Tossing the device onto the dresser beside me, I focus all my attention on her.

"You're not worried?" She glances where it landed. "About Marco?"

"Not tonight, I'm not." Stepping up to her, I lift the thin satin straps of the nightgown and drag them slowly down her arms.

"Oh." Her cheeks flush and she smiles up at me. Even Marco can't ruin what I have planned for her tonight.

"You didn't hide the message from me." Leaning down, I brush my lips across the soft skin of her shoulder, licking my way to her throat. "Such a good girl."

A shiver runs through her as I scrape my teeth across the sensitive little spot just under her ear.

"Such a good girl for daddy," I whisper against her ear.

She moans; it's a guttural sound, and one I'm sure she would rather be able to hold inside, but I feel her, I see her. My girl is a dirty little slut, and she's all mine.

"Look at me, Megan. Don't take your eyes off mine." Once she is looking in my eyes, I drag the straps even lower until the soft cups of the nightgown fall away from her breasts, exposing their beauty.

"I've wanted to do this all night." Releasing the straps, I cup her breasts, lean down and flick my tongue over the peak of one, then move to the other.

"Fuck," she whispers as her hands rest on my shoulders.

I lick her, teasing the peak to get it harder, then I take it between my teeth, delighting in her hiss as I bring her the sweetest sort of pain. As I move to the other breast, I chance a look up at her.

Her lips are wet from being licked, and suddenly I want to be the one tasting them. I'm so possessed by my need for her, I'm becoming envious of even her touching her own body.

Pushing the nightgown over her hips, it falls to her bare feet, leaving her panting and naked before me.

"You're beautiful, Megan. So fucking beautiful." I press my mouth over hers, biting down on her plump lower lip, marking it as mine. I'm starved for her with an impossible hunger that I doubt will ever be filled.

"You sound so angry when you say that." She snakes her hands up into my hair, pulling me down for another kiss.

Enough teasing already, I lift her into my arms and carry her to the bed, tossing her into the middle of it. She laughs as she bounces, and I shuck out of my shirt and pants like some horny teen who can't get out of his clothes fast enough.

She lies back against the pillows as I cover her with my body, again seeking her mouth. I'll never tire of her taste, her scent, her body. Having her skin against mine is unlike anything I've ever felt before.

I've fucked a lot of women. I've even liked a few of them, but nothing compares to being touched by Megan.

Her legs bend, flanking my sides as I sink into her.

Fuck. There's something mind-blowing about being inside this woman. It's like finding my forever home. The world outside can burn to ashes, but inside this room, in this bed, everything is perfect and still.

Threading my fingers through hers, I bring her hands over her head, pressing them into the pillows.

"I might never let you leave this bed." I kiss her mouth, her cheek.

Her pussy stretches around my cock, squeezing me as her body pulls tighter beneath me.

"I can't tell if that's a threat or not." She kisses me back, biting my lip. I try to glare down at her, but she's flushed, she's sweet, and she's fucking perfect.

"No more threats." I drive into her harder, delighting in the little squeal she gives me. "Spread your legs a little more."

She pulls them higher, spreading them wider for me, and I grit my teeth to keep from exploding right there.

"Good girl," I moan eventually, driving into her again. Her wet pussy tenses around me, pulling me into her with each thrust.

Her fingers squeeze around mine as she lowers her feet to the bed. Thrusting her hips up, she meets me thrust for thrust.

"Fuck, Alexander." She moans my name as though it alone gives her pleasure.

This woman is mine.

All mine.

No one will ever hear her moan their name the way she does mine, because she belongs to me. My need for her grows with the knowledge that no man will ever touch her the way I do. No man will ever feel her body wrapped around him and enjoy the pleasure that is Megan.

Because she's all fucking mine.

Releasing one hand, I run my palm over her body, feeling the silky sensation of her skin as I travel down to her hip.

I lift up, just enough to reach between us and find her swollen, wet clit. She lets out a soft moan the moment my fingers flitter across it.

Driving harder into her, I rub her clit in slow circles.

"Fuck," she exhales and pushes her hips farther off the bed. "Alexander, fuck. I have to... please."

"Please, what, baby? What do you need? Tell daddy what you need." Her cheeks flame with the moniker I use, but her pussy tells me everything I need to know. Drenched with arousal, her pussy clamps tighter around me.

"I need to come. Please. Oh..." Her eyes roll when I put

more pressure on her clit and angle my hips to drive even deeper into her.

"You want to come?" I nip her shoulder. "How badly?"

"Please." She squirms beneath me, chasing after a release she won't get until I give it.

"Please, what?" I whisper in her ear, thrusting harder. Fuck me if I keep teasing her, I'm going to explode before I get a chance to hear her say it.

"Please let me come," she whines and it's sweet and sultry and makes my cock even harder.

"Please let me come, what?" I bite down on her earlobe and lean up. I want to see her say the words. Not just feel them.

I've never been one to play into the daddy game, but fuck, when she said it earlier, my balls pulled so tight I thought I was going to make a mess in my fucking pants.

Her pink tongue runs along her bottom lip before she bites down on it. Fuck, she's so fucking angelic the way she's looking up at me. It's too bad for her, she married the devil.

"Please. Let me come, daddy." She smiles softly as she says it, her cheeks brightening with the words.

"Fuck, baby, come. Come all over my cock," I growl as I plow into her. The devil has been unleashed, and there will be no stopping now.

Over and over, I drive into her, hearing her pants and moans that mingle into mine.

"Your pussy feels so damn good wrapped around me." My fingers tighten around hers.

"Harder, please, harder." She pulls her legs up again and I'm lost to her.

Driving deeper into her and harder. "Good girl. Good girl."

"Oh, God, Alexander," she moans, then cries out as her body pulls tight. Her pussy clenches around my cock as she comes unraveled beneath me, pulling me right into the sweet haze of release with her.

"Fuck!" It's animalistic, my roar, but still it leaves me with no relief compared to the explosion of my orgasm.

My chest heaves as I try to catch air, gently releasing her hand and cupping her face.

"Megan Volkov." I whisper her name, placing a tender kiss to the corner of her mouth. "Welcome home."

Twenty-Six

Megan

Mira's cell phone number is a dead end. The same dead end it's been for months. And the text I sent to the last number she messaged me from goes unread. I'm not even sure she's getting them. Maybe she tossed the phone after our last short conversation.

As I walk through the massiveness of Alexander's home, I scroll through her old social feeds, looking to see if she's been active. Of course I find nothing.

Mira has been my roommate for years; we're practically sisters at this point. If something horrible was happening to her, I'd feel it. We can always sense when the other is in trouble. And other than frustration at not being able to get a hold of her, I'm not panicking.

Yet.

A guard stands outside Alexander's office door when I make my way to it.

"Is he in a meeting?" I ask, slipping my phone into my back pocket.

"He is, but you can go in." He pushes the handle that still

has the scratches on it from my ill attempt at breaking in and eases the door open.

"Oh, no, if he's busy, it's—"

"Megan? Come here," Alexander calls from his desk.

When I step inside, three other sets of eyes turn toward me. His brothers, I recognize, but the fourth man is a stranger to me.

"It's not important. I was just wandering...er, looking around. You're busy." I glance at the men. They don't seem at all worried about how long they look at me, unlike the others at the reception last night.

"Come here." Alexander crooks a finger at me from behind his huge desk. The skull vase has been moved from the table in the sitting area to his desk. It's empty this time, making it look even more ominous.

"Good morning, Megan." Kaz grins at me as I approach the desk. His jaw is slightly squarer than Alexander's and there's an amber tint to his brown eyes, but otherwise, he could be his twin.

"Morning." I smile back. Ivan greets me with a soft smile.

I wouldn't bet on him being the nice one after overhearing the three of them talking last night. He's just as ruthless as Alexander, and maybe in some ways worse.

"Oh. I forgot to ask yesterday. How is the waitress?" I ask. "From the club?"

"Vivienne?" Ivan's scowl returns. "She needed a few stitches, but she's fine."

His concrete tone reminds me of Alexander's. Yes, Ivan is definitely not the soft one of the three brothers.

"Ah. Yes. Vivienne." Kaz slaps Ivan's shoulder. "Don't forget. Company ink, Ivan. Company ink."

Ivan's expression darkens. I've obviously picked a wound.

"What does that mean?"

"Nothing." Alexander grabs my hand when I get close enough to them and he pulls me to his side. "This is Lev, a good friend. We were talking about Dexter Thompson."

"The security footage from the party where he died didn't give us any clues as to who fed him the poison." Ivan frowns.

"Maybe it was slipped to him before he went to the party. What was it?" I inquire.

"Potassium cyanide." Alexander answers me without any hesitation.

Only two days ago, he would have ordered me from the office and locked me away for even attempting to get involved in this conversation. Now, he's folding me into the discussion.

"Potassium cyanide? That would act pretty fast. Within ten minutes, I think." Their eyes bore into me.

"Megan?" Alexander tugs on my hand.

"Relax." I grin, squeezing his hand. "I grew up reading mysteries and moved on to true crime when I was in high school. There was a case like that about twenty years ago."

"What happened?" Kaz leans forward in his chair.

"This guy won the lottery, a big winner, and within a few days of collecting his winnings, he died of an apparent heart attack. He had some heart condition, so they ruled it natural causes at first, but his sons thought it was weird, so they ordered an autopsy."

"And?" Alexander prompts me.

"That's when they found the cyanide in his system. They still haven't figured out who did it. His sons think it was their stepmom because she wanted the money to herself. The wife thinks it was his sons because they wanted the money." I shrug. "It's an unsolved homicide."

"If it acts that fast, how can they not know who gave it to him?" Lev questions.

"Not enough physical evidence," I explain. "Since it made

it look like he had a heart attack, no one collected the dishes he'd been using for his lunch—that's when it happened, right after eating. His two sons were in the house and so was his wife at the time, so without being able to prove *how* the poison was given to him, they couldn't prove *who'd* given it to him. So... it's unsolved."

"Much like Dexter. The evidence is all gone by now and without the camera footage to show who slipped it to him, we're back to knowing nothing." Ivan sighs.

"Well, you guys were blackmailing him, right? That's why you have all those boxes with the flash drives and photos? You use it to make people do what you want?" Being Alexander's wife gives me a little leeway here, I suppose. No one's going to threaten to shoot me because I know these things.

"A lot of people could have been blackmailing him," Lev points out.

"Were you told to get everything in the box or only the flash drive?" Kaz asks.

"They wanted the flash drive specifically," I confirm.

Alexander lets go of my hand and opens the top left drawer of the desk. After he rifles around a second, he pulls out the flash drive.

"Maybe something on here will give us an idea. There were a lot of damning things in the box. If they only wanted this, then whoever is involved might be on it." He opens his laptop and pushes the drive into the slot on the side.

The men gather behind Alexander's desk. I scoot a little closer to him, but it's not enough for Alexander. He wraps his arm around my waist and pulls me into his lap.

"I can stand," I whisper, keeping my gaze from seeing the guys' reactions.

"This is better." He winks, then clicks the folder of the drive open.

It's all photographs. He opens the first one.

"Oh, that's Senator McKenzie." Lev chuckles. "Didn't realize he swung both ways."

"Neither does his wife," Kaz says.

"Could Dexter have threatened the senator? Maybe he was trying to blackmail him into something?" I twist to ask Alexander.

"Anything's possible." He clicks through other photos. Some are just scanned copies of contracts Dexter put his signature on; a few are of him at Obsidian. The last photo catches my eye, though.

"Wait." I tap the screen. "Go back to that last one with the woman."

He clicks back a file and there it is.

"That's Cheryl Carmine." I turn in Alexander's lap, feeling his heavy, thick cock pressing against me as I move. My cheeks heat at the sensation.

"Focus, Megan," he whispers in my ear. "Or they'll notice how red you're getting."

I clear my throat and do my best to push it from my mind.

"Cheryl Carmine is married to Stevan Carmine. He owns Cinders Industries, the company I work for." I sigh. "*Used to* work for. That's his wife." I tap the screen with my finger.

"Are you sure? I mean, she's bent over that pool table and everything," Kaz teases, leaning over Alexander's shoulder to get a better look.

Alexander shoves him away, muttering what sounds like an insult in Russian.

"It's her." I nod. "She's not usually wearing all that leather, and the strap-on isn't something I would expect from her, she's so demure and elegant in the office. But it's definitely her."

"There are plenty of photos of Dexter cheating on his wife; why would this one be on here?" Alexander questions. "We've only kept evidence that would ruin him politically and financially. I doubt he really cared if his wife left him or not."

"Especially after seeing those photos with the senator." Kaz laughs.

"I don't know how true it is, but there have been rumors that Stevan is related to some really bad people."

Alexander's grip tightens around my waist.

"What bad people?"

"I don't know. It's just rumors. It is also rumored that if she divorces him, she gets nothing. Not a cent. You can tell she doesn't really like him, the way she looks at him, so there might be some truth to that."

"And I bet if she gets caught cheating, she'll probably get nothing then too," Lev says.

"Maybe whoever was trying to get this drive wasn't looking to blackmail Dexter. Maybe they wanted to blackmail someone else on here, like this woman," Ivan adds.

"Why does it matter who killed Dexter?" I ask.

"It's not the killer I want. It's the person who knew where the information was kept. I want that man." Alexander closes the laptop. "If it's one of my men, it would make more sense for them get the drive themselves."

"Do you have cameras in that room?" I twist to ask him.

"Just one. The footage is taped over after a week."

"So, if he'd been in there and taken it, wouldn't you have seen him?"

"If someone had been watching at that moment." He nods.

"Maybe it's someone who doesn't have access to Obsidian. Someone who would stick out if he was caught in that part of the building." Ivan moves back to his chair.

"That could be true," Kaz agrees, taking his seat.

Alexander pats my hip. "You don't have to sit here for the rest of this. You have better things to do."

I turn around, grinding my ass a little into his cock, because if he's going to get rid of me, he can feel a little discomfort for it.

"Are you telling me to leave so the men can talk?"

He frowns.

"No. I'm telling you that you have better things to do." He looks at his watch. "Like meeting Elana in one hour, and half of that will be spent in the car, so you need to change."

I look down at the brown knit sweater I'm wearing with my jeans. "What's wrong with what I have on?"

"Nothing. It hides your delicious body perfectly from the prying eyes of assholes who don't know better than to look, but you're going shopping with Elana."

"So?"

"Elana enjoys high-end boutiques." He's politely telling me I'm not dressed nice enough to enter their establishments.

"Oh." While what I'm wearing works fine for walking down Main Street, shopping in those high-end stores while wearing a sweater I picked up off the clearance rack last year might not be the right thing. Though I'm sure Elana wouldn't have a problem pulling a *Pretty Woman* moment out of the situation.

"What is she shopping for?" I slide off his lap.

"You. You're both shopping for you. You need a full wardrobe with shoes and jewelry." So, it is a *Pretty Woman* situation.

"I can't buy all that." He's talking about a complete shopping spree. I wouldn't even know how to do that. The largest excursion I've ever been on was back-to-school shopping as a kid. And that included three pairs of pants, a few shirts, and new pair of gym shoes—all bought from the bargain bin.

"You can." He pulls out his wallet, flips it open, and pulls out a black credit card. "Use this."

It's heavy in my hand but sleek and slim at the same time. His name is on the front along with the logo of a Roman-style helmet that's embossed in silver.

"I can't use this, Alexander. It doesn't have my name on it. If they ask for ID—" His chuckle stops me.

"There won't be any issue. You'll have Elana with you, and she's a regular at all these stores. And no one would dare to ask you to prove who you are while you're handing over my card." He sounds so sure of it; I close my fingers around the card.

"So, anyone could steal this from you and the stores would be too afraid to double-check? Isn't that dangerous?"

"Much more dangerous for the person who tried to steal from me." I don't miss the little undertone there, but since he's offering to buy me an entire wardrobe, I let it slide.

"Fine. I'll get a few things, but really, I don't need much." I've never been into fashion. I'd rather go for comfort than look.

"Elana will tell you when you're done." He grins. "She's an expert at this sort of thing."

"You guys seem close even though she didn't grow up here." I'm sure it was awkward for Elana to be around this place.

"We weren't very close when she was little, but when my mother moved to Russia full-time, Elana was always here. She deserved better than the mess my father made for her, but she's never let it get to her."

I can understand that more than he probably knows.

"I think they're waiting for you. I'll go." I start to turn, but he grabs my arm and spins me back to face him.

"They can wait." His lips crush mine in a possessive, needy kiss that I should be used to from him. But I don't think I can ever get used to how overprotective and possessive this man is.

When he breaks away, I run my tongue over my top lip. I haven't been kissed by a large number of men, but enough to know this is different. I'm left dazed and breathless every time his lips brush across mine.

"On your way out, speak with Mrs. Wells and let her know what sort of meals you like. She'll stock the kitchen with whatever you want."

"Even if I want hamburgers for dinner?" I've been craving a good burger for the past two days.

He grins. "Yes, even those things."

Now I'm smiling. "Then I'll talk to her."

"And Megan," he says, grabbing my elbow again when I start to turn.

"Yeah?"

"My sister and you together reek of trouble." He pulls me closer, leaning down until his mouth is just a hair from my ear. "Behave today, or when you get home, I'll put you over my knee before I take you to bed. Understand?"

My mouth dries at his words, but my pussy is another story altogether.

"Yeah. I understand," I answer quietly, hoping the guys aren't hearing us over their own chatter.

"Good girl. Now go." He presses another kiss to my cheek, then lets me go.

He returns to his brothers and Lev with steady, grounded steps — like our exchange did nothing to him. While I slip out of the room, my head and heart somewhere up in the clouds.

Twenty-Seven

Megan

We've been shopping for hours. My feet throb inside my brand-new pair of black Gucci Horsebit loafers. After spending an afternoon shopping with Elana, I stopped asking how much things cost. She would just shrug and tell me to hand over Alexander's card.

I'd let Elana talk me into changing into the dark-olive straight-legged trousers and ivory silk blouse I found at the last store we were at. I'd wanted to keep my ballet flats on, but I lost that battle—just like every other battle waged today.

She hadn't even fought me; she'd just picked them up, carried them to the saleslady, and asked her to get rid of them.

Elana can say whatever she wants, but she is every bit a Volkov.

"I'm starving," Elana announces as she hands over the last of the bags to Artem, our guard and chauffeur for the afternoon. "We're going to walk over to Cafe Spiaggia, Artem. Come join us?"

He looks down the street. "Why don't you get in the car,

and I'll drive you there, then we can all walk into the restaurant," he says while stashing the bags into the back of the SUV.

"It's half a block," Elana protests. "I'll get us a table for three."

He eyes us for a moment, already sensing he's lost. It's Elana after all.

"I'll get a seat at the bar."

"Your choice!" Elana laughs and loops her arm through mine. "Let's go before he changes his mind and throws us in the car."

The street is bustling with people as we make our way across the intersection. Feeling eyes on me, I look over my shoulder and find Artem watching us from the curb.

"He's still there." I tug on Elana's arm.

She sighs. "He'll probably wait until we're inside the restaurant. The only reason he even let us get this far out of reach is because my brothers promised me they wouldn't keep a bodyguard on me."

Once inside the restaurant, we're seated at a table with a small porcelain vase with a single flower.

"Good afternoon, ladies." Our waitress pops up as soon as I have my purse hooked on my chair. Elana rattles off an order before I can even ask for a menu.

"Thanks." Elana smiles at the young woman who hasn't written anything down as she walks away.

"What was all that you just ordered?" I would have been fine with a Caesar salad, but it sounded like she ordered a several-course meal.

"Oh, not much. Burrata for an app, then black truffle risotto, spaghetti with clams, and Tagliatelle alla Bolognese. We'll just put it all out and share. The food here is amazing."

"It sounds like it," I say.

The waitress comes back with two glasses of white wine and disappears again. As I watch her walk away, I find Artem walking in from the back of the restaurant. He takes a seat at the bar where he can see us clearly.

"Artem's here." I take a small sip of the most delicious wine I've ever tasted.

She's on her phone, tapping away and scrolling. Her brows pull tight, and her thumbs fly over the screen.

"Everything okay?" I touch her arm to get her attention.

"What? Yeah." She tries to force a smile, but I know the look.

"Arguing with a boy?" I tease. I want to look at her screen, but I manage to fight off my nosiness.

"No." But she says it with way too much force. "I mean, he's not a boy."

I grin. "Older?"

"Than me? Yes." She looks down at the screen as another message comes through. "He's just being stubborn right now. I need to call him. I'll be right back, promise."

"Of course." I lift my glass while she wiggles her way through the tables to the front of the restaurant. Artem watches her with narrowed eyes but stays perched on his stool.

She must feel his eyes on her because she stays in front of the restaurant window where he can still see her. If she strayed, I'm sure he'd jump off his stool and go after her.

Maybe he would like to be out there with her now, but he's stuck inside because that's where I am. If Alexander really did promise Elana he wouldn't have a bodyguard on her at all times, that means Artem is here because of me.

His jaw is tight, and his eyes are so focused on the window I'm half expecting lasers to shoot out of his eyes at the glass. When his features finally soften, I know Elana has come back inside.

I wonder if she knows Artem has feelings for her.

"Sorry about that." Elana sits back down and puts her phone in her purse. "No more phone, promise."

"Do your brothers know you have a boyfriend?" I keep my voice down to be sure Artem doesn't hear us. Not only because it might upset him, but because he'll tell on her in a heartbeat.

"No." She sighs. "And you have to swear on your life that you will not tell them." She grabs my hand, squeezing it tight. "Please. Promise me, Megan."

I cover her hand with mine. "All right. I won't say anything." I pause a moment. "Do you think they'd be mad or something?"

She chuckles. "Oh, they'd be pissed as hell."

"Because they're so overprotective of you?"

"They just wouldn't understand, that's all." The Burrata shows up and she digs right into the cheese.

"You know, you're twenty-one. You're allowed to have a boyfriend if you want one." I spread the cheese over the toasted bread and slide a piece of roasted pepper on top.

Now this is how you do a snack.

"It's complicated," she says. "It's not so much that I have one, it's who he is. They wouldn't like him."

"Why? Is he like really old?"

She laughs. "No. He's only twenty-six. Not like you and Alexander. A twelve-year difference is a lot."

"It's not so much," I say and pop in the last bite of the toast.

"He's going to be forty before you're thirty. And even if you have a baby right away, he'll be almost sixty when it graduates high school," she points out with a teasing smile.

I know she's joking, just some playful banter. But she's right. He is twelve years older. And I'm not sure I want a baby right away.

Putting my hand over my stomach, I swallow hard. I could be pregnant right now.

"Oh, shit." She reaches over the table and grabs my arm. "I'm sorry, Megan. I was only joking. He's a young thirty-seven-year-old. Hell, I don't think he can even get old; he's too stubborn."

I force a smile, but my stomach is rolling over in a fabulous tornado fashion.

"I scared you."

"No." I shake my head. "I just hadn't thought about it. Everything has happened so fast, and I haven't even really decided if I want to stay married to Alexander after all this mess is over with."

She laughs but covers it by clearing her throat when I shoot my gaze up to her.

"Sorry. It's just... you know Alexander is never going to let you leave him, right?" She leans closer to me. "You're married. There is no divorce option."

"But... his mother left his father, right? She's in Russia?"

"Yeah." Elana nods. "But they were still married. Our father didn't love her, and he still wouldn't let her divorce him. He let her go to Russia, but she was never free from him. Not until he died."

I take another bite, giving myself a moment to think.

"If he wanted other women, why wouldn't he?"

"Because our father was an evil prick," she says with such severity it shakes my soul.

The rest of the food arrives, and Elana arranges the dishes on the table and two fresh plates are settled in front of us.

"So if I want out, Alexander will just send me away?" I watch her plate herself some of the pasta dishes.

"Alexander? No." She takes my plate and fills it with more

food I can even think of eating now with my stomach rolling around like it is.

"Why?"

"Because, Megan." She puts the plate in front of me. "My brother is in love with you. He would sooner lock you back up in that tower room than let you leave him."

My eyes go wide, and she laughs.

"Just because I don't live there most of the time doesn't mean I don't know what goes on."

"But—"

She grabs my arm and squeezes.

"It's okay. He's a lot. I know." She rolls her eyes. "But he wouldn't marry you if he didn't love you. Even if he's too stubborn and stupid to admit it. Maybe he doesn't even know yet. I mean, you're taking your sweet-ass time realizing it, too."

"Realizing what? That he likes me?"

She shakes her head while chewing her pasta.

"Nooo," she says after swallowing. "Not likes you, loves you. And you haven't realized you love him back. But you do. I can see it when you look at him, even when you're pissed. And I know my brother."

Love him?

The background noise of chatter and forks clanking against plates blends into a soundless blur, making my heartbeat the only sound registering in my mind. I sit back in my chair.

Can he have feelings for me?

"You okay?" Elana asks, swiping her napkin across her lips.

"Yeah." I nod, but I'm not. I'm so far away from okay I can't even see okay. "I just need to pee."

I get up from the table so fast my chair almost topples over. The gentleman behind me grabs it before it does and straightens it for me.

After muttering an apology, I search for the restroom sign.

"That way. Just to the left of the bar." Elana takes pity on me and directs me.

Artem is talking with someone when I pass him, but his eyes catch mine. I give him a little shake of my head when he looks ready to bound to his feet, then I hurry to the bathroom.

The bathroom is more luxurious than I've ever seen. This isn't even that upscale of a restaurant. They don't even serve dinner here.

I'm so out of my element.

And not just at this restaurant.

All of this is normal to Alexander. It's second nature for him to have the best clothes, eat the finest foods, have a fucking tower in his mansion for his enemies.

I stare at myself in the mirror at the Alexander McQueen silk blouse and the Andrea Lieberman trousers I'm wearing. I have never in my life owned designer anything, and now everything I'm wearing has a label.

This isn't me.

Friday night pizza and bad movies with Mira on the couch, drinking whatever wine was on sale at the grocery store—that's me.

It's all right.

I can't panic.

After we deal with this Dexter Thompson problem, I'll just have a very calm, very stern, very real conversation with Alexander.

I just need to figure out what conversation it will be.

Taking a few deep breaths and fighting off two more panic attacks, I roll my shoulders back and throw open the door to the restroom. Everything will work out.

Everything is going to be fine.

"Megan Reed? Is that you, dear?" A soft voice pulls me to the left.

I turn, but something thick and rancid smelling is thrown over my head. Before I can lash out, there's a sharp poke in my arm.

Everything's heavy.

And then everything goes black.

Twenty-Eight

Alexander

"He's not even paying attention." Ivan's laugh pulls me from where my mind wandered. Imagining Megan lying across my bed, black rope tied around her wrists and ankles, spreading her body open.

"When you finally get to the fucking point, I'll pay attention." I shoot Ivan a look and adjust myself in my chair. If my cock gets any harder, I'm going to tear through my pants.

"The development agreements will be ready by Monday morning," Kaz says like he's already said it twice.

Maybe he has. I've been busy recalling the taste of my wife's pussy and wondering if we could skip dinner tonight altogether. I'm sure after spending the afternoon shopping with Elana, she's going to need some rest.

And once I'm done with her, she can have it.

"Good." I check the time on my watch. They've been gone a few hours already. Any minute she'll be home.

"The man gets married and now he can't keep one fucking thought in his head." Kaz shakes his head at me with disappointment. "If this is what marriage does to a man, you can count me the fuck out."

Ivan slaps his shoulder. "You'd have to stick to one woman for more than one night in order for marriage to be a danger to you."

"If Kaz ever settles down, I'll give him my Cosmic Starship." Lev doesn't part with his motorcycles easily. Two months ago, he broke every finger on a man's hand because he laid his hand on the bike he was riding that day.

"No. If I ever sell my soul like that, I want the Fighter," Kaz counters. "That thing is sweet."

"That thing is worth more than your soul. It's also a limited edition. It's not for you. You couldn't handle it," Lev tosses back. "You couldn't handle the Harley either, but I'm sure you won't ever get a woman to marry you."

"I can handle a fucking bike."

"Perhaps a Schwinn." Lev grins.

A call from Artem comes through my phone, but when I swipe to accept it, the line is dead. Megan's little icon on the tracking device I put on her phone shows them headed this way. I send her another text asking how things are going.

It's the second text I've sent in the last hour. We need to have a discussion tonight about answering promptly.

A lesson I was sure we'd both enjoy.

"You're going to have to smack him in the head. He's daydreaming again." Kaz's voice rang through.

"Touch me and die, little brother." I shoot him a death glare that only works to entice another arrogant grin from him.

"You could try, big brother."

"This could go on for a bit. Maybe you should just tell us what you found out, Lev." Ivan stands between Kaz and me.

"Found out?" I turn to Lev.

"Yeah. I was just telling them. Your wife's boss? Megan was right, he does have dirty ties. Marco DeAngelo. They aren't blood related, but looks like their fathers fought in the same unit in the Marines back in the day."

"Which makes them practically blood in their eyes, I'm sure." Ivan nods. "You think he found out about his wife's affair and went after Thompson to get him to stay away from her?"

"She filed for divorce a month ago," Lev explains. "Looks like it will be pretty fucking nasty, too. The company your wife worked at is minuscule compared to the other shit he's into. Big real estate guy. Started building luxury apartment complexes out in the suburbs two years ago and they're getting bigger. He stands to lose a shit ton of money if she gets this divorce without him proving she's a cheat."

"Maybe Thompson was a loose end, and she was afraid he'd tell, so she killed him?" Kaz muses.

"I want to know who the fuck was able to tell Megan how to get into Obsidian and where to find the drive. That's the guy I want." My phone goes off again and I swipe it open.

"Alexander... shit... are you there... can you—fuck!" Artem cuts out again. The little hairs on the back of my neck stand at attention.

Megan still hasn't answered my texts, but it looks like she's still with Elana in the car. And they're parking.

"They could be tied together. If her boss wanted proof, and she was fucking Dexter here in the club, this person might know that. It might be time to talk to Mr. Carmine," Lev suggests.

"Fine." I nod. "Bring him in."

"Here?" Ivan's brows peak. "You want him in the pit?"

"Not yet. Just a friendly conversation. But if it goes bad,

there's always the pit." Footsteps fall fast outside the office door just before it flies open.

Elana runs inside, her face flushed, and her hair looks like she's been tugging on it.

"I'm sorry, Alexander. I'm so sorry." She rushes to me.

"For what?" My insides tighten when I look at the door and Megan doesn't walk through.

Artem does, though, and his expression tells me everything.

She's gone.

"Where is she?" I demand.

"I don't know." Elana wipes a tear from her cheek. "It's my fault. I scared her. It was an accident. We were just talking, and then I mentioned your age difference and she got kinda weird. Then she took her purse and went to the bathroom, but she never came back."

I look at Artem.

"Where is she?"

"She never came out of the bathroom." Artem's hands are fisted. "But there's an exit door in that hallway. She could have left through it. When she walked past me to the bathroom, she looked upset."

"I didn't mean to scare her like that." Elana sniffles. "I swear, Alexander, we had a good afternoon. I had no idea she was going to leave."

"Her phone, where is it?"

"I have it." Elana pulls it from her purse. "She left it on the table. If she had taken it with her and grabbed her purse, I would have thought something was up."

"I checked the alley and the street. I questioned the staff. No one saw anything, but it was a busy lunch rush. We were at Cafe Spiaggia. There are no cameras there."

Cafe Spiaggia is known in my world as a safe place to meet out in the open. There being no cameras is deliberate.

"Why would she leave her phone? She would need it." I quickly scroll through her text message history, checking to be sure I haven't overlooked anything.

Nothing that offers any help.

She ran away?

Why the hell would she do that? Especially when there's still danger lurking behind her. This morning, before I tore myself away from our bed, she had snuggled deeper into my embrace and asked me to stay a few minutes longer.

It was the first time in ages that I wasn't downstairs just as Mrs. Wells was pouring my coffee. I'm a man on a schedule, and with one soft little plea from her lips, I'd casually ignored it. All because I wanted—no, needed—more time with her in my arms.

And now she's gone?

"I want men at her old apartment." I clench her phone as I snap the words.

"I already sent them." Artem stands behind my sister. "I tried calling you, but my phone kept breaking up. Before we left the restaurant, I had Sergei and Yogi head over there."

"What did you say to her, Elana?" I level my stare on my sister. Her cheeks are pale and her eyes wide with fear. Of me or that my wife is gone, I'm not sure.

"Elana?" Kaz's voice is softer as he moves to stand beside her. "What happened exactly?"

Elana swallows. "Nothing really. We were talking, and I teased her about your ages. I mentioned having a baby and how old you'd be when the baby grew up." She wiped a tear from her cheek.

"Go on." I temper my voice. Whatever my little sister said may have spooked her, and I need to know exactly what it was.

"I told her that you'd never let her go, even if she wanted a divorce, and she didn't say she did, only that *if* she did." Elana hurries her words. "I told her you love her and that's why you wouldn't let her go."

My chest tightens. "You said what?" There's a tremble in my stomach.

"I told her you love her, and you do." Elana points her finger at me. "I think she only just realized that she loves you back and it might have freaked her out a little. I don't know. All I know is she said she had to pee and never came back."

She loves me back.

I roll the tension out of my shoulders.

"She didn't leave on her own," I say, looking at my sister. "She wouldn't have, I know it."

"What do you want to do?" Lev moves to stand with my brothers and my sister.

"We're going to have a chat with Mr. Carmine. And for his sake, there had better not be one fucking hair out of place on my wife's head when I find her."

"I'm coming too." Elana tries to run after us, but Kaz stops her. I leave him to argue with our little sister.

I have a wife to find.

Twenty-Nine

Alexander

Stevan Carmine's condo is nestled in the middle the Gold Coast overlooking Washington Square Park. As soon as we enter the building, I sense the DeAngelo family presence.

They own a bunch of properties in this neighborhood. I wouldn't be surprised if there were family members behind one of these doors.

"What's the plan, Alexander?" Ivan asks as we approach Stevan's door.

"I told you. We're going to find Megan." As we walk down the hall, I pull my Glock out from behind my jacket and aim it at the door. One quick shot and it's open, making it easier for me when I get to kick the fucker in.

"Now is one hell of a time for him to go off half-cocked," Kaz mutters behind me, drawing his gun to be ready for whatever comes next.

"I'm fully cocked."

A woman dressed in a house uniform crosses into the foyer, sees me, and screams.

"Stevan Carmine. Where is he?" I demand.

"Bedroom," she mutters, unable to take her eyes off the weapon I have trained on her. "Up the stairs and to the left, first... first door."

"Sorry about him," Kaz says as we pass her and head to the stairs. "We'll be just a minute."

Lev stays downstairs with the maid as I take the stairs two at a time.

Moans waft from behind the bedroom door as we approach it. Pleasure filled, erotic groans mingle with the slapping sounds of flesh against flesh.

I don't bother with the knob; I kick this fucking door down too.

A woman shrieks. Stevan is behind her, thrusting into her while she's on all fours. She scrambles away from him, and he falls forward, barely catching himself before landing on his face.

"What the fuck?" He turns to see us, his cheeks pale. "Who the fuck are you?"

The woman presses herself against the headboard, pulling on the sheets to cover herself.

"Go." I nod toward the door, and she leaps from the bed, taking a sheet with her as she runs from the room. Lev will catch her downstairs and keep her contained until we're done here.

Stevan isn't disturbed by having the three of us in the room pointing our weapons at his face. He casually climbs off the bed, grabs the silk robe at the end, and shoves his body into it.

"What do you want?" He ties the robe closed at his waist.

"My wife. Where is she?"

"Who is your wife?" he asks, sounding almost bored.

"Megan Reed," Ivan answers.

"Volkov. Megan Volkov," I ground out.

He pauses a moment. "Alexander Volkov. Yes?" He gestures to me as he walks to the nightstand, grabbing a pack of cigarettes and pulling one out.

"Where is she?"

He lights the cigarette and blows a cloud of smoke up at the ceiling.

"I have no fucking idea."

"She used to work for you."

"A lot of people work for me. Why would I have her?" He takes another drag, letting the cigarette dangle from his mouth as he walks to the other side of the room.

"I don't think you're understanding the trouble here." I squeeze the trigger, and his cigarette disappears from his mouth.

Stevan freezes, his entire body locking up for a moment before he slowly turns back to face me. What's left of the cigarette butt drops from his mouth when he opens it.

"I don't have your wife." His voice drops, and finally, he's realizing I'm willing to blow his fucking head off if he doesn't have the answers I want. "Really. I don't know who she is."

"Your wife is fucking around behind your back. You need evidence to the fact, so you don't lose your balls in your divorce. So, you have your friend Marco get her involved in a fact-finding mission. Is any of this ringing any bells?" I move the barrel of my gun to aim at his balls.

His face twists at the mention of Marco. "Marco's behind this?"

He doesn't sound like a man talking about a friend. There's more disgust in his tone than anything else.

"You should tell me everything you know." I don't move my gun, and I'm getting impatient.

"I don't know anything. Cheryl is a fucking whore; she's been fucking anything that moves for years. I don't give a shit, but then she files for divorce and wants half of everything. No fucking way." He sinks on the bed, sitting at the edge.

"Go on," I urge.

"Right after she filed, Amelia Thompson shows up and tells me she knows my wife's been fucking her husband. I ask if she has proof that I can use, and she says she'll work on it. That's all I fucking know. Her husband dropped dead a week later, and I haven't seen her since."

Slowly, I lower my gun. Dexter's fucking wife took him out.

Poison is generally a woman's weapon.

"So, you never got the proof you needed?" Ivan presses.

"No, but I told Cheryl I had it or was going to get it. It was a fucking fight; I don't remember exactly what I said."

"When was that?" Kaz asks.

"Right after Amelia and I talked."

"And where is your wife now?"

"I have no clue. Probably swimming around some sewer like the other vermin in this city. But she has a condo in Lincoln Square; she could be there."

"And Marco? He plays into this somehow. What's his involvement?" My finger's getting itchy. If I can't shoot this asshole, I need to find somewhere to put my anger.

The longer this all takes, the longer Megan is sitting somewhere with people who want her hurt. Or dead.

My teeth snap at the idea. I can't lose her.

I will not fucking lose her.

"Other than he's been fucking my wife too?" He half laughs. "I don't care what you do. Shoot him, sell her, just leave me out of the whole thing." He swipes a hand through the air.

"I want the address," I tell him.

"I'll get it. You get in the car and start heading that way." Ivan taps my shoulder. "I'll text it."

Kaz is right behind me as I jog back down the stairs. Lev

stands in the living room, with both frightened women sitting on the couch, staring up at him.

He puts a hand in the air, letting me know he'll stick around with Ivan as we pass through.

"Get a hold of Sergei," I tell Kaz as we climb into the SUV, me behind the wheel. "Tell him to go through those photos and the drive again. Cheryl knew we had that photo of her; that's probably when she went to Marco for help. Maybe there's someone else in those photos, someone else at the club she's been screwing around with that might lead us to whoever told her how to get into the records."

Kaz gets right on it, tapping away on his phone while I peel out into the street.

The sunlight is already starting to fade. I may not know exactly where my woman is, but I know one thing for fucking certain.

Anyone who's put a finger on her is going to fucking pay with their life.

And by the time she sleeps tonight, she will be home.

Our home.

Thirty

Megan

It stinks in here.

The tower room Alexander had me locked in that first time was uninviting, but it didn't reek of piss and blood. This jail cell I'm in now does.

My head still throbs on the left side where a large swollen knot has bloomed. Probably from when I was dumped onto this concrete floor.

"Hey. Anyone there?"

I sit up from the wall I'm leaning against. The door to the cell is made of bars and the hallway is dark. As far as I knew, I was alone down here.

"Yeah?" I hurry to the door, pressing my cheek to the bars so I can look down the corridor as far as I can.

An arm slides out into my view and her fingers wiggle. "Can you see me?"

"Your hand, yes."

She laughs. "Oh, good. I'm really alive."

I take a deep breath. Having someone there brings some

relief to the terror I've been drowning in since waking up in this darkened pit.

"Are you all right?" I ask.

"I hurt in a lot of places, but everything's working. I'm so glad you're here."

"Where is here?" I hesitate in my question, not sure I really want to know.

"I don't know exactly. I hear trains now and then that sound like the subway, but I haven't been outside. And they only take me upstairs when they want to..." her voice trails off into a sniffle. "I'm fine. Did they hurt you when they brought you in?"

"No. Not really." I touch the bump on my head. It's nothing, I think, compared to what she's been through. "Do you know who has us?"

"Michael DeAngelo." Her voice hardens with the name. "This is his place. He runs things here."

"Michael?" I rest my head against the bars. "He's related to Marco?"

"I've heard him talk about Marco. I think they're brothers," she says.

"Does anyone know you're here?"

"I doubt it." She snorts. "I've been here over a week."

"And Michael brought you here?"

"No, not him." She yawns and I wonder what time it is. There are no windows to the outside, and it's been dark in here since I woke up.

Something crawls over my foot, and I jump back a step. A squeak echoes against the wall and a small dark shadow runs between the bars and down the dim corridor.

"Who was it?" I remember the voice in the restaurant. It was a woman, and I can almost place it, but every time I get close to it, the throbbing in my head starts again.

"He didn't give his name before he snatched me off the street. I was walking home from the bar; it was dark and I was alone. Never even heard him coming. The only thing I really remember about him was his voice. Really raspy and he had a thick accent, not Italian."

My skin electrifies. "Was it Russian, you think?"

"Could be." She sighs. "How'd you get here?"

"I was taken from a restaurant." In the middle of the afternoon in a crowded restaurant. Someone had to have seen it. Artem must have noticed right away I didn't come back from the bathroom.

"It's going to be all right." I bolster my voice. "My husband is going to come; he's going to get us out of here."

Alexander isn't going to let anyone hurt me. He will burn the city to the ground to find me.

I sink back to the ground, pressing my back against the wall I share with my new roommate.

"He'll find us."

"Well, I hope he has an army with him," she says with a bitterness to her tone. "There are at least twenty men upstairs right now."

A door creaks open, cascading our little cells in bright fluorescent lighting. I wince from the discomfort and turn my head to the side. It's too much at one time.

Clicking of heels against cement tick off each step our visitor takes as she makes her way toward us. The light shining behind her keeps her face hidden from view.

It's only when she steps up to my door that I catch the whiff of her stuffy perfume. I know this scent; it's like a blend of stale rose mixed with the damp musk of old fabric. And I've only ever known one person to wear it.

"Cheryl?" I blink until my eyes adjust to the lighting, and then she comes into focus.

"Hello, Megan." Her thickly painted lips spread into a wide grin. She's wearing a deep-green dress with a white pearl necklace. Her red hair is swept up into a French twist and pearl droplets dangle from her ears.

"What's going on?" I wrap my hands around the thick, chilled bars. The grime and dirt of the place covers them.

Cheryl sighs. "You have something that I need. Once you give it over, you'll be free to go."

"I don't understand. What do I have?"

"The flash drive." The facade of pleasantry drops with her demand.

"I don't have it," I say quickly.

"You saw it."

"I don't have it anymore. They took it from me." She has to know the Volkovs are never going to give over that drive. And knowing that could make her desperate.

Life experience has taught me being desperate makes people do really stupid things.

Like sneaking into a Russian Mafia's secret club office to seek out blackmail information for the Italian mob. I can mentally flog myself later for my previous stupidity, but first I need to get out of my current mess.

"Then we'll have to figure out a way for you to get it back."

"You want me to steal the drive from my husband and hand it over to you?" Hopefully, she'll hear the insanity inside the statement.

"Since he's your husband, it should be an easy thing to accomplish." Her smile twists as her eyes roam over me. "You're a pretty thing, I'm sure you can get him wrapped around your little finger easily enough."

"Alexander Volkov," I deadpan. "You think he's dumb enough to fall for something like that?"

"He was dumb enough to think marrying you would keep you safe," she snaps.

"I'm not doing it." I grip the bars of my door tighter. "You and Marco can go fuck yourselves. I'm not doing anything else for him."

She runs her tongue over her top teeth, then lets out an exaggerated sigh with a shrug of her shoulders.

"You really are a stupid girl. When Marco suggested having you get the drive, I told him you'd fuck it all up, and you did."

"Hey. I'll go. I'll get whatever you need," the woman in the cell beside me pleads.

Cheryl leans to the left, trying to peer into the second cell. When she can't quite get a good look, she walks over to her door and pulls out a key from the pocket in her dress. The door creaks eerily as it swings open, and a small woman steps out.

She's young, barely eighteen if that, and naked. Bruises cover her arms and legs, purplish handprints on her thighs. A scab has formed over a deep cut on her left breast and her hair is pulled up into a set of pigtails, exposing the dark bruises around her neck.

My stomach rolls at the thought of what she's been through at the hands of the evil in this place. Of what horror awaits me if Alexander doesn't get to me.

"I can do it. I can get what you need." The young girl shifts from one foot to the other, folding her arms over herself. More to keep herself warm than an attempt at modesty. She lost that long ago, I think.

"You could use a shower." Cheryl makes a face and takes a small step back. "Those assholes don't care where they stick their dick."

"Alexander will never allow anyone near those files. He has them hidden." I try to make her see reason, but I'm not sure where it's going to get us even if she does decide to give up on her search.

"Cheryl! Are you down here?" Footsteps hurry down steps and the lights flicker to life.

My stomach twists.

Oleg.

I remember him from the wedding dinner. He'd been one of the last in a long line of well-wishers. He shook Alexander's hand and congratulated him on our marriage. Alexander introduced him as one of the men who's worked with him for a long time.

A fucking traitor!

He stands at the foot of the stairs for a moment, taking in the girl standing in front of Cheryl, before swinging his gaze to me. His eyes widen when he sees me.

"What the fuck is she doing here?" he nearly bellows, rage filling his expression.

"I told you I need that drive. If Stevan gets a hold of those pictures, I'm fucked."

"I said I had it handled," Oleg nearly growls.

"You haven't handled anything. Marco gave Michael the okay to help us. If she won't get the drive, we'll trade her for it. That Volkov bastard won't let his wife be harmed." Her face flushes with irritation.

"Do you have any idea what you've done? The hell you're bringing down on us?" He steps forward, his hands flexing at his sides. "When Alexander finds out what you've done, he won't rest until he's killed everyone in this house. Including you."

"Then I guess you're going to have to use your big Russian muscles to protect me." She sneers.

Oleg's jaw tenses. He looks in my direction, then at the young girl. Hanging his head, he shakes it.

"You've been the worst mistake of my life," he mutters, then snatches the key from her. I step back from the door when he forces the key into the lock.

"Oleg." I put my hands up to ward him off as he swings the door open.

"What are you doing? You can't let her go!" Cheryl reaches for the door, but Oleg shoves her back.

"You're not fucking thinking." He taps his temple as he rages at her. "The Volkovs aren't a little fucking problem. If she has so much as a scratch on her when she gets returned to them, they will hunt down everyone associated with the DeAngelo family. Including you. Including me."

"Then she doesn't need to be returned," Cheryl states casually, pulling out a small pistol from the deep pocket of her dress. It fits perfectly in her palm as she aims it at me.

"And how will you get that fucking drive, then?" he demands. "All of this over a damn divorce settlement. This should have been easy. A simple blackmail, but you fucked it all up."

"Then I'll fix it. We'll get rid of her, you'll take care of my husband, and it's all done." She pulls back the hammer, loading the chamber.

I step farther back into my little cell. There's nowhere to hide in here. Nothing I can use to shield myself from her aim.

"I said I can help. Let me help!" the girl starts yelling. "Leave her alone!"

"This crazy bitch." Oleg turns just as the girl runs into Cheryl. The gun goes off and a chunk of cement flies past my ear as the bullet lodges in the cinder blocks of the wall behind me.

Cheryl scrambles up to her knees as the young girl reaches for the gun, but Cheryl aims and shoots quickly. The young girl flies back. Blood sprays across my face as she hits the ground inside my cell.

"No!"

"You idiot! You couldn't stop a little girl?" Cheryl turns her fury on Oleg, but he's preoccupied.

He's at the stairwell, listening.

I fall to my knees beside the young girl. The bullet hit her in the neck, and I push my hand over the wound, trying to stop the blood from pouring out. It seeps between my fingers. It feels hopeless.

Pale-blue eyes look up at me, blinking away tears.

"Fuck! Please, help us!" I scream. It can't end like this for her. Not when she's so close to getting free of these monsters.

Cheryl stares down at what she's done and pales.

Oleg curses, looks back at us, then runs up the stairs. Men's shouts echo when he opens the door at the top. A shot rings out, then another.

"Oh no." Cheryl looks at the gun in her hand. "No, no, no." Turning on her designer heels too quickly, she trips a little, catching herself on the wall as she makes her way to the stairs.

More shouts, more shots.

"You're going to be okay. It's okay." I remove my hand from her neck so I can pull off the blouse I bought only hours before. Balling it up, I press it against the wound. "It's okay."

I have no idea if I'm right. If she'll survive this.

She's so young.

"Please be okay," I whisper to myself.

"What's that?" Her voice is strained when she asks as another shot goes off.

I smile down at her as a tear rolls off my cheek.

"He brought an army."

Thirty-One

ALEXANDER

"Where the fuck is my wife?" I shove a man against the wall of the living room, putting the barrel of my gun against his neck. "Where is she?"

He pisses himself.

"You fucking pussy." I step back as his piss streams out of his pants and pools near my shoe. "Where is she?"

"W-which one is your wife?" he questions with terror in his eyes. This man isn't a member of the DeAngelo family. He's just one of their fucking customers.

Low-life pieces of shit that come here and pay Michael for the use of whatever women he's keeping in his stables. Rage fills me. If one of these motherfuckers have so much as looked at Megan, I'll have their eyes.

And then I'll have them skinned and left to wallow in pain until they finally die.

"Black hair with two white stripes." I press my gun harder into his throat. "Where?"

"Fuck," he winces. "I don't know. She hasn't been up here."

Men scream in another room just before shots ring out and bodies drop. These assholes deserve slower deaths than what they're getting.

"Where's Michael? Marco!" I continue my interrogation.

"Not here. I swear." A bead of sweat rolls down the side of his red face. "I swear, I don't know where they are. They're not here."

"Alexander! Here!" Kaz yells from somewhere near the back of the house.

The man I'm holding pales. He may not have touched mine, but he's in a house of depravity even I can't defend. And if he'd had the chance, he would have done whatever he wanted to Megan.

For that, he dies.

Releasing him, I step back and deliver one single shot to his throat. His eyes go wide with surprise as he grabs at the wound, already gurgling and trying to find air.

He slides down to the ground, and I step over him. He'll be dead in a matter of seconds.

Jogging to the back of the house, I step over bodies and pass my men as they're taking care of others in this disgusting place. Clearing out Michael's house is a clear message on where I stand with the DeAngelo family.

As I move through the house, one of my men run straight into me from a hallway.

"Fuck. Sorry." Oleg stands before me. Artem and Kaz rounded up the men on this mission, so I'm not positive who's here, but I haven't seen Oleg since the wedding dinner.

"Did you find Kaz?" I question him.

"No, man. But I think he's back there. I heard him yelling a second ago." He points down the hall I'm headed. "I was going to check upstairs."

I pause, staring at him. Something's off. His gaze doesn't completely catch mine.

"Alexander! I found her!" Kaz's bellow steals my attention. I leave Oleg where I found him and run to her.

"This way. Down there." Boris waves at me from a small room off the back of the kitchen. "Kaz went down already."

I barrel my way down the cement stairs into the tiny area under the house.

"Megan!" I shove two of my men out of the way when they're blocking me, and I rush forward.

Megan is sitting on the dirty concrete floor inside a makeshift cell with a bloody naked woman lying in her lap. She's holding a wadded-up shirt against the girl's neck.

"Megan." I step into the cell. Kaz looks up at me from where he kneels on the other side of the girl.

"She's been shot," he tells me.

"She won't wake up." Megan's tear-stained face turns up at me. "She was trying to protect me, and she got shot."

I look at Kaz.

"There's still a heartbeat, but it's faint. She needs to get to the hospital," he tells me.

By the looks of the girl, the gunshot wound might not be the only reason she needs a doctor.

"Megan, you have to let her go. Kaz will take her." I lower my voice so she isn't spooked and squat down beside her. Blood covers her chest and is smeared across her cheek.

Between all the dirt and the blood, I can't tell if she's hurt or not.

"Okay." Megan nods. "Okay, but be careful. They hurt her a lot. Please be careful." She looks to Kaz.

"I got her." Kaz gently slides his arms beneath the frail girl as Megan releases the pressure on her neck.

As Kaz makes his way out of the cell and back up the stairs, Megan gets to her feet.

"Are you hurt?" I grab her arms and lift them up so I can see her torso. There's no bruising on her stomach or chest, but there's so much blood.

"I'm fine." She assures me. "It's her blood."

I grab hold of her, hugging her to me. "You're sure?"

"You came. I was so afraid you wouldn't be able to find me." She wraps her arms around me, burying her face into my shirt.

"I told you; I will always find you." I clench my teeth, holding back the emotion threatening to escape.

Until I had her back in my arms, I didn't allow myself to consider how close I was to losing her. But now that I have her, I can touch her, smell her, kiss her, I realize I was only a moment away from never holding her again.

"But I left my phone at the table," she mutters into my shirt. "The tracker was in my phone."

"You knew about the tracker?" I lean away so I can look into her beautiful face. Even with the dirt and the blood, no one can compare to the beauty I'm holding.

She gives a wary smile. "Alexander. I'm not an idiot. You've been tracking me and mirroring my phone this entire time. You are an overbearing, overprotective, arrogant man."

A tear rolls down her cheek, and she quickly swipes it away.

"And I've never loved you more for it." She presses her cheek into my chest again.

"You love me." I squeeze her tighter.

"And you love me," she says. "In case you didn't already know. I know how stubborn you can be."

Even with the horrors surrounding her, she finds a way to goad me.

"Let's get you out of here and home." I release her and quickly take off my shirt. "Put this on."

"It's too big." She shakes her head.

I lean forward. "Megan, you're standing here in your bra. Put on the shirt."

It's as if she just remembered she'd taken off her shirt to help the girl. A blush blooms beneath the smears of dirt, and she grabs the shirt from me, shoving her arms into the sleeves and pulling it over her head.

She's swimming in it.

Perfect.

Realizing she's barefoot, I swoop her up into my arms.

"I'm fine. I can walk," she argues, but it's a pathetic attempt. She lays her head against me and wraps her arms around my neck at the same time.

"When we walk through the house, keep your eyes closed, baby," I warn her as I climb up the stairs to the main floor.

"You killed them?" She snuggles into me.

"Yes."

"How many?"

"All of them. Now hush. Let's get you out of here." I kiss her forehead and take the last step up into the house. Other than my men, no one else has survived the night. The place is in ruins, bathed in the blood of my enemy.

Once we're outside, Ivan catches up to me.

"Cheryl. We have her," he tells me while his eyes roam over my wife. "She okay?"

"She's fine," Megan mutters, her annoyance at being talked about like she's not right here showing.

"Good." Ivan gives a nod. "Cheryl. What do you want done with her?"

"Bring her to Obsidian," I order as I carefully place Megan in the back of my SUV.

"What about Oleg?" she asks, letting me buckle her in.

"What about him?" I ask.

Her eyes widen. "He was helping her. He was the guy on the phone," she tells me.

My skin ices and I look over my shoulder at my brother. His expression darkens.

"I will find him," he promises and stalks away.

The bastard was right in front of me, and I let him walk away. He was acting weird, and other than his appearance at my wedding dinner, I haven't seen him in weeks. I should have known something was up.

"Alexander." Megan touches my arm. "Can we go home now? Please?"

I cup her face, wiping away the dried blood and dirt.

"Of course, baby." I climb into the SUV beside her and tap Artem's shoulder.

"Home."

Thirty-Two

Alexander

Megan's asleep when I get home, so I'm quiet as I cross the bedroom to the bathroom. When the light shines on her face, I take another beat to watch her sleep.

Her hair's pulled up into a ponytail, so I can see every inch of her face. I've never found so much peace by looking at anyone the way I do her.

Afraid to wake her, I step into the bathroom and shut the door. My muscles ache as I strip out of my clothes. Mostly my knuckles, but they'll heal.

The fucking bastard won't.

After turning on the hot water, I step beneath the stream, washing away the dried blood from my hair and skin. It swirls around my feet.

"Alexander?" Megan's voice carries through the bathroom, and I open my eyes beneath the stream to find her standing just outside the glass doors of the shower.

Stepping away from the hot water, I open the door. She

takes a look at the red-stained water on the floor and then to the pile of clothes at her feet.

"Ivan found him, then?" She toes the bloody shirt.

"He did." I wipe my hand down my face, getting the water away from my eyes. "You were asleep. Did I wake you?"

"No." She folds her arms over her stomach. She's wearing one of my shirts again. It's been three nights since I brought her home and she's taken to sleeping in my clothes.

I don't mind. Seeing her wearing my things fills me with peace.

A peace a man like me doesn't deserve.

"Is he dead?" She looks up through dark eyelashes, like she's not sure she really wants to know.

"He is." I flex my hand, my knuckles are already swollen and bruised. It will look only worse in the morning.

She steps to the shower, picks up my hand, and brings it to her lips. Gently, she kisses each swollen knuckle.

"You killed him." She steps into the shower with me, the water spraying her immediately, making the shirt stick to her skin.

"You're not angry?" I brush my hand over her hair, partly to inspect the egg-sized bump. It's down to the size of a marble now, and at least she doesn't grimace when I graze it.

"He brought girls to that place," she says. "I think he brought that girl there."

"Sharon?" The seventeen-year-old who nearly died in my wife's arms after saving her life. She had a hell of a battle that night, but she pulled through.

"Yeah. She called this morning. She's home now. With her parents."

"I know." I wanted to be certain they knew the men involved with hurting their daughter had been taken care of. That not a single one of them was left with air in their lungs.

253

She takes another small step toward me, pushing me into the stream of hot water.

"Of course you do. You know everything." She runs her hands over my shoulders, across my chest, and down my abdomen until she reaches my heavy cock.

It's been hell not touching her these past few nights, but I needed to be sure she was all right. I needed to be sure my rage was fully contained so I wouldn't hurt her in its stead.

Her hand wraps gently around my thick shaft and squeezes.

"Fuck, baby." I push my head back into the spray. "Tighter, baby, squeeze tighter."

She kisses my chest, licking away the water running down between my pecs. Her fingers tighten, making me groan.

"Did you make him suffer?" She lifts her eyes to mine with her question. The innocence I enjoyed so much the first time I saw her is still there; it's just hidden beneath the darkness of what she's experienced.

"I did." I won't lie. By the time he drew his last breath, he was begging for death to take him. What I couldn't break with my fist, I tore open with my knife. "He hurt you. He deserved it."

"He wasn't the one who took me." She presses her body against mine, letting the shower soak her.

"No. The man at the restaurant was one of Michael's men." His hands were removed first for daring to touch what's mine. "Oleg betrayed us, he's been working against us. He put you in danger. He deserved everything that happened to him."

She looks at me, a sad smile on her face.

"Just promise me we won't be using his skull as a centerpiece in the dining room?"

I laugh.

"No. He wasn't worthy enough for that."

"Good." She slides down my body, stopping only when her knees hit the floor and she's eye level with my cock.

"Megan." I touch her cheek, directing her to look up at me.

I'm breathless as she drags her eyes up to mine, opening her mouth and bringing my cock to her lips.

A curse in Russian escapes me as her tongue darts out, licking the bead of precum from the head. This woman will be the death of me if she keeps this up.

I press my hand to the wall of the shower as she tightens her hold on my shaft and lowers her attention to the underside of my cock. From balls to head, she runs the flat of her tongue, and my eyes roll from the waves of pleasure pulling my balls tight.

My moan echoes in the shower as she wraps her full, pretty lips around my cock and sucks me down deep.

"*Ya sobirayus umeret.*" And it will be a happy death.

She takes me even deeper and my eyes roll. I can't take much more of this. My balls are already pulling up hard and ready to explode.

Sinking both my hands into her hair, I fist it, pulling her back until her mouth pops off my cock. Even the little popping sound makes me want to unload.

"Never tell me how you learned to do this so well." I move one hand to her mouth, running the flat of my thumb along her bottom lip. Water sprays across her face from the stream behind me and I can only wonder how pretty she'd be with my cum dripping from her cheeks.

Hooking my thumb into her mouth, I open it wide.

"I've killed enough men this week." I plow back into her mouth, hitting the back of her throat in one thrust. She swallows hard around me, which only makes it better for me.

She mutters around my cock, and the humming of her attempt to speak vibrates down to my balls.

"Fuck, baby. Fuck." I rock my hips and push deeper into her throat. When she looks up at me, tears mingle with the shower water sliding down her cheeks. The sight brings me that much closer to losing it.

She flicks her tongue along the underside of the head, and I break.

"Up." I pull free from her warm, loving mouth and reach down for her, sweeping her up to her feet and shoving her against the shower wall.

"But I—" I silence her protest with a kiss. Her hands press against my shoulders, her fingers curling into my flesh as I lift one leg and line my cock up with her pussy.

I nudge her chin until I have her eyes focused on mine. Stray hairs that have fallen out of her ponytail stick to her cheeks, thanks to my manhandling. Her lips are slightly swollen from stretching around my cock. And all I want to do is plow into this woman until we both explode, but first, I want the words.

She hasn't said them since the night I found her in that fucking cell, and I need them again.

I need her to hear them, too.

"I love you, Megan." I push my cock against her entrance. "I would kill every man on this planet to keep you safe. I need you to know that. I need you to understand you're safe with me. I will love you until the world ends."

Not even death would change my feelings for this woman.

"I know, Alexander." She smiles. "I love you, too. I can't explain it and I don't want to even try. You make me crazy, but I've never felt as safe, as loved as when you're holding me."

My throat constricts at her words. I'd only wanted three of them, but everything she's given me has electrified my soul.

I seal my lips over hers and thrust my cock into her. She

moans against my mouth, her lips parting and letting my tongue fuck her mouth while I pin her to the shower wall.

Her leg hooks around my hips as I drive into her, fucking her until she's crying out from the pleasure I give her.

When she comes, her head rolls back, and she cries out. The little moans and gasps ricochet off the shower walls. Her nails dig into my shoulders as I find my own release.

The ecstasy of my orgasm is nothing compared to the heaven this woman has brought into my life. With all the drama, the danger, she dragged love into the light.

What was dark and untended is now bright and thriving.

I press my forehead to hers, gently putting her leg down and letting the spray of the water pelt my back.

"I will never let you go. To do so would kill me."

She wraps her hands around my neck.

"I love you, Alexander. And I'm not going anywhere."

Thirty-Three

Megan

He's back to being a complete overbearing ass.

"You have to help me here, Elana. If I don't get out of this house, I'm going to lose my shit." I follow her around the living room as she does her best to ignore me while texting her little boyfriend.

"If I help you, Alexander will put *me* in the pit." She spins around so fast, I don't have time to stop, and I barrel right into her. "Is that what you want?"

My abduction has scared Elana into never taking me out of the house again. While I'm grateful for the concern, I need to get out of here.

I could threaten to tell her brothers about her secret boyfriend, but that would just be low. Besides, she'd know I was lying.

"Of course not. And he wouldn't, by the way," I point out. "He's closing off that room down there."

He wants no violence in our home. Somehow, the man still thinks he can put me in a cage to protect me from the world.

But since I won't have to worry about what horrible things are happening down there, I'm letting him.

"You're as impossible as your brothers." I plop down on the couch and pull out my phone.

"I would hope so. She's a Volkov after all." Alexander stands in the doorway, arms folded over his chest and a heated glare settled on me.

"Good, you're home. Entertain your wife. I have plans." Elana pats Alexander's shoulder as she passes.

"Who are your plans with?" he calls after her.

"None of your business!" she yells back.

"Artem will drive you." He turns to confront her as she hurries to the front door.

I don't need to see her to know she's rolling her eyes at him.

"The DeAngelos are still a problem," he reminds her.

"Yeah. Yeah. He can drive me. But he stays in the car!" The door slams shut after her demand, and Alexander's shoulders drop.

"Between you and my sister, I'm going to become a cranky old man before my time."

"You mean you aren't now?" I tease from where I'm lounging on the couch. "Seriously, Alexander. I need to be useful. I need to get out into the world. I know the DeAngelos are angry, but let's face it. There's always going to be someone who hates you."

"Thanks." He frowns. "But you're right."

"You don't need to sound so grumpy about it. You agreeing with me was bound to happen."

"I'm not grumpy." But his frown intensifies so he doesn't really pull off the lie.

"If you say so." I'm learning which battles to pick, and this isn't one of them. Especially if I want him to open the prison door for me.

"I've decided to let you go back to work." He puts a hand up before I can even react. "But not at Cinders Industries."

"Okay." I push up from the couch and go toe to toe with my husband. He may dwarf me with his size. He may make the ground shake with his glare. But I'm standing my ground.

"First of all, you don't allow me, Alexander. That's not how this is going to work. Second, I wouldn't ever want to go back to work there. Besides, Mr. Carmine is still grieving his wife's suicide." I smirk.

"You saw that, did you?" His eyebrow arches.

"I get the news on my phone, of course I saw it. Potassium cyanide in her martini? It was clever."

"She was overwhelmed with guilt from killing her lover." He shrugs like it's all just a big game.

"I'm not sure how you got anyone to believe that, but I'm just glad you're on my side." I sigh. "Now. About the 'allowing me comment.'"

"I know. I used the wrong words, but the sentiment is the same. Nothing's changed here—"

"Megan!" someone yells my name from the foyer. "Megan!"

"Who is that?" I step around him and hurry into the foyer just as I'm tackle-hugged and fly back into Alexander.

"Megan! Oh, thank God! Are you all right?" Mira pulls back from me with just enough space to look me over.

"Mira!" Emotion fills me, making it impossible to get any words out beyond her name.

"You look okay. I'm so sorry. But you have to help me! He's a barbarian. And crazy! He's insane!" She catches a glimpse of Alexander, and her mouth drops open. "Holy shit, you're just as massive as him."

"As who?" I ask, grabbing at her arms, trying to make her settle down. Her panic is palpable.

Alexander gets between us and pulls Mira off me.

"What is going on?" he demands.

Another figure walks through the door Mira threw open when she arrived.

"Rurik," Alexander says.

With a severe frown and a deep crease in his brow, Rurik steps farther into the foyer, taking in the scene before him. Alexander is practically holding Mira up with one hand and me steady with the other.

"Alexander, I would appreciate it if you got your hands off my wife."

Continue reading the Vicious Sinners Series with Book 2, Devious Madness.

About Measha Stone

Measha Stone is a USA Today bestselling romance author with a deep love for romantic stories, specifically those involving the darker side of romance, all the possessive dominant heroes, and their feisty heroines. If you love a well deserved happily ever after, you will enjoy her books.

www.meashastone.com

Also by Measha Stone

DARK ROMANCE STANDALONES

Valor

Kristoff

Dolly

Finding His Strength

Simmer

The Mob Boss' Pet

Gray

MAFIA BRIDES

(Staszek Family)

Taken By Him

Kept By Him

Captivated By Him

RELUCTANT BRIDES

(Kaczmarek Family)

Unwilling Pawn

Reluctant Surrender

Veiled Treasure

INNOCENT BRIDES

Corrupted Innocence

Ruined Innocence

Ravaged Innocence

Surrendered Innocence

Savored Innocence

Defiled Innocence

SACRED OBSESSION

Sacred Vow

Solemn Vow

Unbreakable Vow

OWNED AND PROTECTED

Protecting His Pet

Protecting His Runaway

His Captive Pet

His Captive Kitten

Becoming His Pet

Training His Pet

EVER AFTER

Beast

Tower

Red

Hound

Siren

GIRLS OF THE ANNEX

Daddy Ever After

Obediently Ever After

DARK LACE SERIES

Club Dark Lace (Boxset)

Unzoned

Until Daddy

BLACK LIGHT SERIES

Black Light Valentine Roulette

Black Light Cuffed

Black Light Roulette Redux

Black Light Suspicion

Black Light Celebrity Roulette

Black Light Roulette War

Black Light Roulette Rematch

Windy City SERIES

Hidden Heart

Secured Heart

Indebted Heart

Liberated Heart

Daddy's Heart

Windy City Box Set

Made in United States
Troutdale, OR
07/08/2025